T0195734

Legacy of a Free Spirit

Lisa Allen Thompson

AuthorHouse™
1663 Liberty Drive
Bloomington, IN 47403
www.authorhouse.com
Phone: 1-800-839-8640

Published by AuthorHouse 01/09/2015

ISBN: 978-1-4969-6326-0 (sc)
ISBN: 978-1-4969-6327-7 (hc)
ISBN: 978-1-4969-6325-3 (e)

Library of Congress Control Number: 2015900354

CONTENTS

ACKNOWLEDGEMENTS

I humbly, gratefully, and respectfully, thank all artists, musicians, and writers, I have quoted or wrote about in this book. You are my heart and soul and lifeline. With sincere appreciation I acknowledge Ms. Pricilla Meier, my elementary school teacher, who published my first creative works and encouraged me to keep writing. I honor my cousin/ soul sister, Heather St. Clair, for her writing and art that continues to inspire me, and shares my passion for the arts and humanity. With love and light I recognize Bill Chace and Nancy Fraga. Bill for his tireless and sometimes relentless determination to see this book completed is worthy of acknowledgement for its very existence. Along with his beautiful soulmate, Nancy Fraga, they are the best friends and best fans any artist could hope to have. To the Connecticut band DiamondBack, I remain dedicated and thankful for your phenomenal talent. I will always remember that it was your music and songs that inspired me to pick up the pen I put down long ago and started writing again. Aerosmith: For the song, "Dream On" (and everything else you ever recorded!)I have carried that song in my heart for forty years! I further acknowledge Tom Laughlin, Delores Taylor, and Warner Brothers, for the movie Billy Jack. It's as relevant today as it was back then, and planted the seed in my creative soul that I may someday use my creativity and human services for the human good. To my Family and Friends, for which I am Blessed to have the very best, I remain thankful for the love and light you bestow upon my life.

This Book is Dedicated to:

~My Grandchildren~

Rebecca Elizabeth

&

Luke Mark

May you always have a song in your heart, love and light in your soul, and live in peace and harmony.

"Suddenly, all of my ancestors are behind me. "Be still", they say. Watch and listen, you are the result of the love of thousands."

-Unknown

MERMAID

~ *Destiny Sinclair* ~

It was a beautiful night in the waters of Aquidneck. The full moon lit up our home around the Isle of Manisses. The bluffs and shore were magnificently crystalline in twinkling blues, lavenders, pink and white. The granite, white quartz, rose quartz and clay mirrored over the sea like radiant jewels.

Always held under the full moon, are our Sovereign Sisters of the Sea Society gatherings. All the area mermaids, from Watch Hill, Mattoonuk Neck, Conanicut Isle, Mystic Shores, and our Isle of Manisses, gather to celebrate in solidarity our sisterhood and enjoy cakes and wine. After much merriment we adjourn with our Mermaid Blessing:

"Send us now to live in peace, Oh, Mother Moon, of earth and seas, In heart and soul, we're love and light, And do what's good and do what's right." ~Bright Blessings~

Mermaids are very whimsical at play and very philosophical in everyday life. We are free spirits and fiercely independent. However, in love, we are the most loyal and equal partners, and as mother's, we are very loving and devoted. And right now, this partner and mother of three needs to get home to her partner, Gus, and three beautiful daughters: Charity, Hope and Grace.

Upon arriving home, I heard the sound of drumming in the air, and saw fire light on the isle. It appears the natives of the land are having a celebration tonight also! The natives of the land hold many of the same beliefs we merfolk do. We are all one in this big circle of life. They believe as we do, every living thing has a spirit, a soul, and a reason for being. The circle takes us from birth, death, and rebirth. In between death and rebirth, we mermaids believe we go to the Summerlands to rest, the natives of the land believe they rest with The Great Spirit. Here, during life, our purpose is to live in harmony and peace, or the circle of life will unravel, and cease to be evermore.

My family are all in slumber as I arrive home and I check on each of them before retiring myself. Gus, my soulmate, is an inspiring musician and prolific songwriter. (I, Destiny, the poet and songwriter, am also passionate about music and song!). Charity is our peacemaker, and already dedicated to preserving harmony with the land and the sea. She has many muses, her favorite are the whales, our record keepers, and a great wealth of knowledge regarding creation and history. Also, the dolphins who are great teachers and communicators, the doves who teach love, forgiveness, and inner peace, the owls provide great wisdom, and the eagles teach about freedom and justice for all. She also is attentive to the teachings of the wolves, who teach finding your own path and loyalty, and the deer, who teach kindness. Gus and I hope we mentor her well also! Hope has an innate way of making one feel better with her mere presence and appears to be a natural healer. She enjoys learning the healing properties of plants. Some of her favorites are: rosemary, lavender, dogwood, heather, hemp and sweet grass. Rosemary, is sometimes called "the dew of the sea" and good for remembrance. Lavender, sometimes called "the elf leaf" promotes calmness and peace. Dogwood is good for granting wishes, (a mermaid trait) and Heather, good luck and protection. Sweet grass is useful for calling up the spirits, and hemp, the most natural medicine of all, heals an assortment of ailments. Grace is our little clairvoyant and very psychic. I believe she has been around the great circle a few times, to the Summerlands, and back again, an old soul! She has alittle mojo bag of crystals, stones, shells and feathers. Her favorite stones are: aquamarine, sacred to the sea goddess, and moonstone, sacred to the moon goddess. Additionally, her very favorite, star sapphire, a very useful stone for psychic work and spiritual understanding.

Merfolk celebrate eight holidays a year which we call "the turn of the wheel". Tonight, we are celebrating Imbolc. The days are starting to grow longer and beginning to grow warmer. The isle is once again thawing and becoming green after a long cold gray season. The merfolk gather around for opening ceremonies:

"Lord and Lady, Thank you for this night, The wheel turns once again, And we are Blessed with love and light." ~ Blessed Be ~

The wee one's ring little bells and sing and dance for us. Gus played his guitar, and we all joined in singing and dancing all evening. Charity, Hope, and Grace love hearing family stories and learning of their heritage, and Imbolc was a favorite. The Goddess Brigit, is honored during this holiday. She is the Goddess of creativity and also of Scottish heritage. The wee one's are of Scottish heritage on my mother's side of the family and we all aspire to be creative, so Brigit is special to us. Brigit can sometimes be seen in the form of a beautiful white swan swimming around the Scottish Isle's. Scottish decent mermaids are known for their love of music and have beautiful singing voices. They are especially known for being kind and granting wishes! There are mermaids who exist who are tricksters, and witches, and sirens. And they do bad things! They are bitter and negative, and are indeed revengeful if crossed. However, most mermaids are peacemakers and very compassionate. We live by a simple set of rules:

"Mind the Threefold Law ye should, three times bad, an' three times good."

"Fairly take and fairly give."

"And it harm none, do what ye will."

Mermaids are also firm believers of karma!

"Oh, my stars!" Another full moon is upon us! Time passes so quickly. It's time again for our Sovereign Sisters of the Sea Society gathering. We enjoy our cakes and wine while making our final preparations for the upcoming Ostara concert. Merfolk love our music! We are expecting a big turnout this Ostara, and decided the cummaquid of the isle would serve best. We adjourn with our Mermaid Blessing and then it was merry meet and merry part.

Alas! Ostara! What a beautiful day we have to celebrate! The days and nights are in equal balance at this time, and it's warmer, and the flowers are budding, some in bloom. Excitement is in the air as all the merfolk gather for the concert. We have an exceptional show this Ostara with some known artists! Stephanie is the opening act, the ancient queen of music! The other female performers are, Janis, a real rocker who always leaves us with a piece of her heart, and Bonnie will play that slide guitar and sing with that soulful voice, and Melissa will leave us wanting to come over for more! Some of the male bands came up from the southern shoals. One of Gus's favorites is Duane! Duane is the master of strings and plays many a guitar! Duane is a legend in the guitar world. The Free Birds are here too! Their music and songs remind us to follow your heart and nothing else, and be something you love and understand. The Boys from Beantown Bay, from up northern waters, are playing too! I've loved their music since they began years ago and always will! I don't know where time goes sometimes! It just goes by like dusk to dawn!

After the concert we all tried to wind down and enjoy our cakes and wine, and felt Blessed to have shared an afternoon of music and song, and another turn of the wheel. And now:

"Lord and Lady, Thank you for this night, The wheel turns once again, And we are Blessed with love and light." ~ Blessed Be ~

"Send us now to live in peace, Oh, Mother Moon, of earth and seas, In heart and soul, we're love and light, And do what's good and do what's right." ~ Bright Blessing ~

Sovereign Sisters of the Sea Society adjourned. Beltane celebration and ceremony plans in order!

It's a beautiful evening under starry skies. The days have been growing longer and it's balmy. We are celebrating with the natives of the land. They have planted their crops and are calling upon the Great Spirit to help provide sun and rain for a bountiful harvest. And as with every turn of the wheel, we merfolk, will thank Lord and Lady for our many blessings. The isle people, the natives of the land are very respectful of the living circle.

They believe every living thing has a spirit, a soul, a reason for being. It is demonstrated in their way of life. If they do sacrifice a living thing, it's for survival. They receive it with blessing and great thanks to the Great Spirit. A white tail deer, a moose, or a bear, will provide clothing, shelter and food. The skins will also provide the skins for drums. Antlers and bones may provide tools. Hoofs make good rattles used for music and ceremonies. A tree, provides shelter, tools, a canoe, and its wood is used in fire for warmth, cooking, and worship ceremonies. Wood is also used for an instrument used by the natives that makes the sound of the whistling wind. Fir branches are very good for bedding. Stones and shells provide tools for work and cooking. Clay from the land is useful for pottery and grasses for baskets. Plants provide food and medicine. The natives of the land also make beautiful jewelry with stones and shells from the sea. Even the feathers of a bird are used for clothing. The natives waste not a blessing given to them from the Great Spirit and they take nothing from the circle of life without giving it honor and thanksgiving. The natives of the land and we merfolk gather together in a circle as the ceremony begins. We provided wreaths of flowers and the natives have made a fire and play beautiful music. The drumming and the wood whistling flute lay peace upon us while the rattles call up the spirits for worship. The natives share with us another ceremonial rite, the passing of the pipe. The stem of the pipe is made of wood and beautifully decorated with a carved stone bowl at the end that hold the leaves from which we smoke. Smoking it in a circle represents the great circle of life. We end the ceremony with the natives giving a Blessing in their Algonquion language to Great Spirit. After a moment of silent meditation we give thanks as always:

"Lord and Lady, Bless us, day and night, And as the wheel turns once again, Keep us in your love and light." ~Blessed Be ~

The natives of the land and we merfolk are happy to share in worship as we all believe it doesn't matter how you worship, as long as you live in harmony with respect and honor of the circle of life.

Welcome our full moon and another gathering of the Sovereign Sisters of the Sea Society. Litha is approaching when the sun is at the highest point in the sky and provided us with a warm evening, air and sea. This is also a popular time for two loving hearts to join together in union in a ceremony called hand-fasting. This year two of our Sisters, Luna and Starr, are making that commitment, and tonight we are honoring them during our meeting. We are showering them with love and light, and as usual have plenty of wine and cakes for the celebration. As a gift we have presented them with a conch shell engraved with their names. A conch shell is often associated with the Goddess of Love, Venus. Legend is Venus was created from the union of sea and sky. Venus was born of sea foam and water, and came to the circle of life upon a conch shell. The two mermaids were so happy we thought of this gift to represent their union of hearts. We merfolk believe any two hearts can join in union: mermaid and merman, mermaid and mermaid, or merman and merman. A union, or a family, is love and light, and respect and honor of each other, in any relationship. Merfolk believe in healthy relationships where both partners are equal and always bring out the love and light in each other. One partner never controls or takes power in the relationship! We wish Luna and Starr many happy turns of the wheel together and adjourn our meeting.

"Send us now to live in peace, Oh, Mother Moon, of earth and seas, In heart and soul, we're love and light, And do what's good and do what's right." ~ Bright Blessings ~

I think this turn of the wheel is one of the largest in celebration here at the Isle of Manisses. Merfolk tend to travel more when the days are long and warm and enjoy coming to visit our isle waters. It's wonderful seeing our merfolk neighbors from surrounding areas near and far. Some have come over from Watch Hill, Mattoonuk Neck, Conanicut, and Mystic Shores, and from further up, Georges Bank, Grand Banks, and Flemish Cap! We have family visiting from Sable Isle, Deer Isle, Isles of Shoals, Appledore Isle and Star Isle! Gus and his band are providing the music tonight and there will be much singing and dancing in this lively throng of merfolk! Fruits of the season, blueberries and strawberries, will add extra flavor to our delicious cakes, and some cool sweet mint tea for drink.

The Sovereign Sisters of the Sea Society have once again gathered under the full moon, however, it is a quick meeting tonight! Alas! We have two full moons in a short period of time, and the second one is called the Blue Moon! The Blue Moon is a most magickal time for us Mermaids and is celebrated with great honor to divine sisterhood! So, merry meet, and merry part.

Blue Moon! The most magickal moon! The mojo bag of nights! Tonight the Sovereign Sisters of the Sea Society celebrate our divine sisterhood and solidarity. This is a special occasion celebrated by all ages, Maiden, Mother, and Crone. My family is hosting the Blue Moon celebration and we have chosen Beavertail Rock at Conanicut Isle for the ceremony. We are all dressed in our best white attire. Always white for Blue Moon celebrations! And all adorned with our favorite shawls, flowers in our hair, and our favorite stone. My favorite as always, my star-sapphire necklace and rings, and silver hoop earrings. Charity chose aquamarine, Hope amethyst, and little Grace chose moonstone. Great Grammie Orpha, and Grandmother Elizabeth have not arrived yet but we are waiting in anxious excitement. We have a Grandmother Betty also, who is Grandmother Elizabeth's mother, but, she won't be joining us this celebration. She is a good grandmother, however, she is also the quintessential gypsy soul and is always traveling! The Blue Moon hung so low in the sky it appeared to be dancing on the waves of the sea as we begin the ceremony. Great Grammie Orpha opened the gathering with a few words of wisdom and this song:

"Be king to auld grannie, for noo she is frail, As a time shatter'd tree bending low in the gale. When ye were bairnies tott, totting about, I watch'd ye when in, and I watch'd ye when out…"

My heart filled with love and light listening to her sing! An old Scottish song, so fitting for our family, and this ceremony, as she represented the Crone stage of life. She will soon be called back to the Summerlands, and I so cherish every minute I get to spend with her and will carry her memories when she is not in my sight, until we meet again!

"…When the gloaming o' life comes like mist o'er the glen, Then be kind to auld grannie, for noo she is frail, As a time shatter'd tree bending low in the gale." -Archibald Mackay

Grandmother Elizabeth and myself represent the Mother stage of life. And we have chosen music and song for celebration. First a dance, as we all gather in a circle, Maiden, Mother and Crone. First we danced deosil, and circled about, then widdershins, and circle back again. And then in song:

"…And when your time with me is spent, If I have done nothing else at all, I'll be content, If I have only done two things, Given you roots, given you wings…" -Ellen Cannon Reed

The teen Maidens performed a play about the Goddess Gwenhywfar. Gwenhywfar is the mermaid goddess! She represents the strenghth to make good choices in our life. Not to be led by emotion or ruled by reason, but to live in harmony, in a happy balance.

Next the wee ones, also Maidens. They have chosen to do a play about Goddess Diana! Diana, is the divine feminist!

After cakes and wine and much merriment with our Sisterhood of Mermaids, it was merry meet and merry part.

"Send us now to live in peace, Oh, Mother Moon, of earth and seas, In heart and soul, we're love and light, And do what's good and do what's right". ~ Bright Blessings ~

As the wheel turns again, it is now Lughnasadh, and the days are growing shorter and it is cooler at night. It is the beginning of the harvest season and we celebrate with a shared meal in the merfolk community. It is very foggy for our celebration tonight and a cool mist is hanging over the sea, but it doesn't dampen our spirits. We are warmed with the love and light of our unity and the warmth of a bonfire. However, our celebration is shortened by the flash of light in the sky and the rumbling sound also coming from up above.

"Lord and Lady, Bless us day and night, And as the wheel turns once again, Keep us in your love and light". ~ Blessed Be ~

The Sovereign Sisters of the Sea Society are gathered tonight many leagues under the sea in the waters of Aquidneck. It is a full moon but not visible to the eye. Another storm appears to be about the isle and this one is fierce! It has lit up the skies with flashes of light and sending bolts of light down to the sea and land. The wind is tossing the sea about and sending waves crashing to the Isle of Manisses, pounding the shore and the bluffs. Also pounding and crashing is the sound from the sky. Tonight, the Sovereign Sisters of the Sea Society have no time for cakes, wine or merriment! We have gathered together to summon up all our magickal powers if needed during this storm. Mermaids, have always been known for their great service to those in need, and we are prepared. "In heart and soul, we're love and light, And do what's good and do what's right".

The light and darkness are again in balance and a cool wind is blowing across the waters. It is Mabon and harvest time. We celebrate this turn of the wheel with the natives of the land. They have harvested their crops in preparation of the coming cold season. We will not see much of the natives during the cold season as they try to stay inside their shelters as much as possible. Tonight, however, we share a great thanksgiving of the season, honoring harvest. We sit in the traditional ceremonial circle for the celebration. We merfolk have provided foods from the sea and the natives have provided a bounty of harvest foods. Before our feast of sea foods, apples and gourds, pumpkins and squashes, berries, corn and smoked meats, the Shaman gives the Blessing and thanks to the Great Spirit, for our meal we are about to receive. And accordingly, we end our ceremonial gathering with the natives of the land passing the ceremonial pipe, in peace, unity, and promise to live in harmony in the circle of life. And with every turn of the wheel:

"Lord and Lady, Bless us day and night, And as the wheel turns once again, Keep us in your love and light". ~ Blessed Be ~

Once again, under the full moon, the Sovereign Sisters of the Sea Society are united. We are very busy planning for our most sacred holiday and turn of the wheel, Samhain! Samhain is a time when we honor our ancestors and the veil is very thin between the circle of life and the Summerland. Samhain Eve we have a great formal ball, and

Samhain Day is spent in quiet meditation. Many preparations and planning, cakes and wine, and:

"Send us now to live in peace, Oh, Mother Moon, of earth and seas, In heart and soul, we're love and light, And do what's good and do what's right". ~Bright Blessings ~

Gus looks so handsome in his formal attire, although Charity, Hope and Grace have a case of the giggles, as they are far more used to their daddy in his casual bohemian style. I look one more time in the mirror and adjust the wreath of flowers in my hair, and check on my silver jewelry. I have on my usual black, my favorite color of choice for dressing up. Charity, Hope and Grace are settled in as we walk out the door. Grandmother Elizabeth is here to care for them and they cherish time spent with her.

Gus and I dance the night away and all in attendance are merry and gay! Gus sat in with the band for a few songs, which is always a crowd pleaser, and pleases Gus too! Cakes are abundant in all flavors, shapes and colors, and the wine flowed! On the way home Gus and I stop for some quiet time under the bluffs. We sang some of our favorite songs together, and to each other, and shared how Blessed we are in love, and life!

I have prepared an altar with beautiful branches of brightly colored leaves from the season. Pumpkins, chestnuts, acorns, and apples are also put in place with great care. Tonight, we honor our ancient ones, our ancestors who are at rest in the Summerlands. They are close by tonight. Very close, as the veil is thin! Merfolk spend this sacred holiday in quiet meditation at home with their families. Unlike, the other turns of the wheel, where we usually gather in great celebration with food and song and merriment, this is a sacred day, and a time for quiet reflection and honor.

"Lord and Lady, Bless us day and night, And as the wheel turns once again, Keep us in your love and light. And to our loved ones, in the Summerlands, Very near to us tonight, You are always in our heart and soul, And in our love and light". ~ Blessed Be ~

The Sovereign Sisters of the Sea Society are meeting under the full moon, however, I have been excused this meeting. Yule is approaching and Gus and I have to prepare for our celebration here at Isle of Manisses, and visiting my family across the waters, at Mull Isle and Isle of Iona. Gus and the wee ones are in quiet slumber so I slip out to honor Mother Moon in her fullness under the bluffs in quiet solitude. The waters of Aquidneck are a peaceful calm tonight and the full moon and stars are twinkling in the sky and the sea. A gentle snow is falling and adds to the white light and magick of the night. I decided to take a quick trip to Watch Hill and sit on my favorite rocks by the sea there. I have a bit of Grandmother Betty in me sometimes as I too can be a bit of a loner and have a gypsy spirit! Watch Hill has always been a peaceful place for me and it is beautiful tonight, as always!

"Send me now to live in peace, Oh, Mother Moon, of earth and seas, In heart and soul, I'm love and light, And do what's good and do what's right". ~ Bright Blessings ~

I returned home beneath the full moon and twinkling stars, with the snow still falling gently, in the white magick of the night, feeling blessed and at peace.

Yuletide is the holiday of love and light and quite possibly the most joyous turn of the wheel. Much merriment and lots of visiting to and fro with family and friends. Tonight we gather with our merfolk community around Isle of Manisses. The celebration site is so festive with a beautiful arch of greens and mistletoe with silver bells. Pine boughs are also all about with bright red berries and adorned with silver, red and green ribbon, and in the center the traditional bonfire. Simple handmade gifts from heart and hands, are exchanged with love and light. The true meaning of the season being love and light, not material wealth or material things, but, the spirit of giving from the heart! Gus leads us in holiday songs playing his guitar, and others have musical instruments as well, and we all sing out in love, light, peace and harmony. The wee ones are especially merry and gay and dance and sing along.

"Lord and Lady, Bless us day and night, And as the wheel turns once again, Keep us in your love and light". ~Blessed Be ~

Morning has broken and it's a bright sunny day for traveling across the waters to the Scottish Isles! It's such a beautiful place! In the warm seasons the glens and valley are lush and green, with beautiful wild flowers in full bloom and color. My favorites are the heather on the hills and the bluebells. The cliffs of the highlands resemble the bluffs here at Isle of Manisses. It is equally beautiful in the Yuletide season also and I am anxious to get there! The wee ones are also excited and can't wait to arrive, and all along our travels are asking when we will arrive and are we there yet! Gus and I are engaged in conversation but I paused for a moment to check on the wee ones as it had grown quiet and I haven't heard their usual chatter and giggling. Just as I suspected, they were up to something, as I look to see Charity, Hope and Grace straying from our route of travel! They confessed they were curious and following the sound of jingle bells. As I summoned them back I taught them a lesson about the sound of jingle bells in the Scottish waters. What they heard was a character known in these parts as the Shellycoat! He is a well known prankster and his favorite prank is getting others lost! The jingling sound is his coat of shells. I advise them to stay close to Daddy and Mommie, and to behave! We hadn't gone much further when we were again abruptly stopped by the screams and giggles of all three wee ones. In extremely shrill and frightened voices they tell me there is a monster following us. I look back and note something is indeed rapidly approaching us. Upon further inspection, although the water is a bit murky, I note large flippers on a long large creature. And as it got closer, I recognize it is Nessie! Nessie has been a friend to many generations of Sinclair's! She lives in the Loch and although very large and very mysterious she has never been known to hurt a living thing. She is quite the legend in the Scottish Isles. We stopped and visited with Nessie for a spell and she was thrilled to meet another generation of Sinclair's, our little Gracie, Hope and Charity. I invited her to come along with us and we were again on our way. As we arrive, I hear the bagpipes, and see the family awaiting our arrival. Friends, family, Nessie, and a few folks from Brigadoon, all gather for a festive Yuletide celebration. We join in gay merriment with singing and dancing and cakes and wine, much like the Isle of Manisses, only here in the Scottish Isles we have ale and bannock cakes. And bagpipes! As the bagpipes played we sang in unison my favorite song of the season, Silent Night:

"Samhach an oidhch'; Naomha an oidhch', Saoghal 'na chadal; 's a-mach bhoar soills'..."

These are the joyous and precious memories of a family being together. I will have them always in my memory and heart and soul.

"Cadal gu neamhaidh seimh, Cadal gu neamhaidh seimh".

Scottish mermaids are known for their love of music, family and friends, and especially for granting wishes! My wish for all tonight is: may you always have a song in your heart, love and light in your soul, and live in peace and harmony.

All the area mermaids are once again gathered together under the full moon for the Sovereign Sisters of the Sea Society meeting. From Watch Hill, Mattoonuk Neck, Conanicut Isle, Mystic Shores, and our Isle of Manisses, we are gathered in sisterhood and solidarity. We have been doing so many moons and many trips around the sun. We live in love and light, and peace and harmony, within the great circle of life. We believe in being of service whenever we can and love to make wishes come true. Mermaids are dedicated to this legacy!

"Send us now to live in peace, Oh, Mother Moon, of earth and seas, In heart and soul, we're love and light, And do what's good and do what's right". ~ Bright Blessings ~

PILGRIM

~ *Rebecca Allen* ~

Save our souls, I think this must be the coldest and most fierce winter of my lifetime! The snow seems to fall endlessly but for the most part is bearable. However, the ice and wind remain relentless! I stoke the embers and add a log to the fire so we all don't freeze. Well at least, me and the children, as usual Seth is not at home! Most likely at the Towne Tavern with his manly friends and lady friends, although he will tell me he was working late again! Due to the storm he will likely stay at his friends home at Shady Creek Farm, out of necessity of course, even though the truth be known, if he had come home from work as most family men do, it wouldn't have been necessary! I wrap my shawl around my shoulders and sit by the fire before retiring. It has been such a long hard year and I am growing weary and tired. Since Mother passed away last summer, Father has taken up with the town trollop and has been making bad decisions and will probably lose the family farm. My marriage is a mockery and there is much gossip and whispers of Seth's clandestine affairs with women and involvement in some kind of dishonest business and prejudicial town government. My mind drifts to where it all began…

I was born Rebecca Allen. The Allen's have always been a respected family in Ashville, being one of the founding families of the settlement. My family was very involved in government and social affairs. It was a town social where I met Seth Thomas. His parents owned the village blacksmith shop where Seth also worked, and our parents were friends. When Seth and I started courting I think it was already decided by our parents that we would marry. The town has gone through many changes since then. My family has slowly withdrawn from town affairs as it has been turned into a who you know law government, not fair law government, and my family refuses to compromise our respected integrity in association. The Selectmen, The Constables and Magistrates appear to run operations on more of a monetary value and not moral values. It worries me too that Seth seems to have become a part of this way of thinking! We can't have a government that is run by a misuse of power and authority because they are more prosperous than the working class. The children are getting older and I do not want them to bear witness to the whispers and gossip of the town regarding their father. I have grown tired of it all! The mockery of the marriage is not what I want my children to perceive as normal. Seth's drinking and bad temper are also out of hand and I do not want Luke or Lyssa to grow up thinking any of this is socially acceptable! I have a decision to make.

I awoke to find it was the first light of day and I had spent the night in my chair! Luke and Lyssa are awake and I give them some coffee and warm cornmeal with molasses for breakfast. I added some beef, parsnips, carrots, and turnip to the broth in the kettle and prepared to make some bread. Seth never did come home last night but has arrived for his noontime meal. I attend to my wifely duties while the children spend some time with their father. After eating Seth needs to return to the blacksmith shop but promises the children he will see them later for supper. I have my doubts about that and wonder how much longer I can keep finding excuses for Seth who continues to fail to keep promises to the children, and me!

As I expected I lie to the children as I am feeding them supper and tell them their father has to work late again. After the evening chores I put them to bed and I too lay myself down to sleep in my own bed. I was awoken to the sound of Seth stumbling into the room as I pretend to stay asleep. I don't know what is worse, knowing Seth is not at home at night, or having him come home smelling of alcohol and cheap perfume and hoping he does not touch me as a husband to his wife! Luckily, as usual he lands on the bed and just passes out.

The children have had a fun day playing out in the snow and come in and hang their wet clothing to dry. I warm them both up with a hot meal and warm piece of pie. They inquire where their father is and I tell them he is busy in town. I know full well where Seth is! Probably drunk at the Towne Tavern with his cohorts or entertaining a young lady at Shady Creek Farm! I read aloud to the children and then tucked them into bed for the night. As I was thinking about going to bed myself, Seth has come through the door and is demanding his supper. I served him the pork and beans from the crock that were still warm from our supper. He began shouting at me that I had not fulfilled my wifely duties and this meal was not fit for a working man and man of the house. I tried to ignore him as I could tell he was drunk and did not want to upset his bad temper. I gave him some warm coffee and a piece of pie in silence.

In anger he gets out of his chair, bangs the table with his fist, and then knocks the table to its side and everything on it goes crashing to the floor. Now Luke and Lyssa are awake! Seth continues in drunken rage not caring the children are awake and witnessing his behavior, which he does not feel is unwarranted, as he throws me outside with no overcoat out into the snow and bolts the door! I could hear the children crying and pleading with Seth to let me back in to the house. After a fashion the door opened and there were my two precious children telling me to keep quiet and come in. Seth was passed out in drunken stupor on our bed and I went up into the loft and slept with the children. I cannot let this continue! All I could do was pray right now: "O God, who has drawn over weary day the restful veil of the night, wrap our consciences in heavenly peace. Lift from our hands our tasks, and all through the night bear in thy bosom the full weight of our burdens and sorrows, that in untroubled slumber we may press our weakness close to thy strenghth, and win new power for the morrow's duty from thee who givest thy beloved sleep. Amen." Tomorrow is another day. We never speak of Seth's behavior and act like a normal happy family.

My best friend Olivia lives out on the shore with her husband Garrett and son Noah. Garrett is of the Dalton family, a good and respectful family, who own the Dalton Mercantile, The Dalton Shipyard, and Sojourn Inn, in Scituate. She has told me many times, in fact pleaded with me, to come for a visit and consider living with them or at the inn, and start a new life with the children away from Seth! I have been thinking now may be the time. Divorce is a sin and a scandal and I haven't wanted to put the children through it, but, it is not right they should live this life either! Although, this house and land was part of the family farm, I will have nothing but my clothes and Luke and Lyssa when I divorce, as Seth owns it all by law of marriage. He has also threatened to keep the children if I even consider divorcing him. He is quite cocky in his ways since becoming one of the throng amoung the Selectmen, the Magistrates and the Constables, and knows he will easily get his way by way of advantageous associations! And the fact women have no rights! I pray to our Lord every day to give me the stenghth to endure and help me with this difficult task before me.

As Luke and Lyssa and I enter Scituate we are greeted by the smell of the sea air and a warm spring breeze. We are almost to the home of Olivia, Garrett and Noah as we pass by the wharf and the children note the Dalton name on many buildings and are excited we have arrived. Olivia and Garrett have a beautiful home with a large front piazza overlooking the sea and surrounded by a split rail fence and beautiful hydrangea and wild flowers. As we travel down the laneway I can see Olivia and Noah out on the sprawling lawn awaiting our arrival. The children laugh and play and Olivia and I share a long embrace. Jillie comes out to help us with our trunks and greets us all affectionately also. Jillie is from Jamaica and has been of help to Olivia since Olivia was a young girl, and never appears to age. Jillie and her family have been part of Olivia's family for three generations now. Our belongings gathered we enter the house and Jillie places our trunks in the bedrooms where we will stay and Olivia serves us tea and shortcakes in the front sitting room. The afternoon flew by as Olivia and I catch up on each other's news. Garrett has arrived home and also greets Luke and Lyssa and I most welcomingly. We enjoyed a grand dinner of pheasant, and vegetables and warm bread in the dining room and the children and I are already more at ease in the pleasant surroundings of our friends company. My children and I retire early as we are tired from the long trip and for the first time in a long time I sleep soundly.

I awoke to the sound of the sea outside and the smell of coffee drifting up from the kitchen. I was the last one downstairs for breakfast but quickly joined in for some delicious warm porridge that Olivia had made. She had prepared warm cornmeal topped with cinnamon, nutmeg and warm molasses that was also a favorite at the Sojourn Inn, the locals calling it Hasty Pudding Porridge. Along with my hot coffee it was again a treat to be served a meal and be relaxed in a family atmosphere. Olivia gathered the three children and set off for a day of play and fun. After helping Jillie clean up and finishing some kitchen chores we decided a fiddlehead soup might be tasty for dinner tonight. Fiddleheads are plentiful in the spring and Jillie and I walked outside to the wooded area with two large baskets to gather some.

Another day has passed too quickly as we all enjoy our fiddlehead soup for dinner. Jillie, Olivia and I all had a hand in preparation putting the fiddleheads to simmer with some onions, potatoes and carrots and then finishing it off with some heavy cream. After our meal Jillie offers to put all the children to bed and Garrett, Olivia and I move into the front sitting room for some peachy and adult conversation. I noticed Olivia looked a bit tired and pale and shared my concern with her. She insisted she was just fine, however, I noted the frown and look of concern on Garrett's face telling me she was not. We continued to talk about life in general and then Garrett brought up some disturbing news from town. Apparently there has been some hysteria regarding people doing "the devils work" and reports of "witches" in Salem. Warrants have actually been issued to people with different ways of worship or ways of thinking and local Magistrates were holding them in prison awaiting trial, standing accused! Garrett further reported that the prisons are allegedly in cruel order and the accused are living in squalor and unfit conditions. Some others in fear of being accused or under suspicion haven taken to hiding in the woods! The religious and political disharmony in some of our towns has become alarming! When did we start imprisoning people with different ways of worship or lifestyles? And why does it appear there is a growing tendency of town officials governing from personal gain and using misuse of authority to create a likewise society where law is decided by coercion of compliance rather than moral and ethical principles defined by law? My mind drifts back to Ashville. And what is to become of me and my children when I divorce Seth and try to get justice under that kind of governing? I dread going back to Ashville, and Seth!

I hadn't opened my eyes yet but could already tell it is another beautiful day here in Scituate. The sun was warming my face and I felt the early morning sea breeze as it filled my room with refreshing salt air. The waves are gently rolling in and out washing the shells, stones and sand in rhythmic sound as the gulls make themselves known in candid harmony. Luke, Lyssa and I arrive downstairs to find Jillie and Noah already outside at play and an industrious Olivia has prepared two rhubarb pies for tomorrows Sabbath Day at the meetinghouse. Olivia again appears pale in color and looks tired, but, I don't mention it. Garrett left for town early this morning, but before leaving suggested to Olivia that the ladies and children enjoy a day seaside, and then meet him later at the Sojourn Inn for dinner, and we all agreed it was a wonderful suggestion! Luke, Lyssa and Noah skipped, jumped, ran and frolicked around the rocks and in the sea foam. We all collected some seashore treasures and keepsakes and enjoyed a lovely lunch prepared by Jillie. Another peaceful and relaxing day at the seashore!

All dressed in our Sunday finest we went down to the village for worship and fellowship at the meetinghouse. All is quiet in the village and wharf as all work ceased at sundown last evening and will continue peaceful until sunset tonight in observance of the Sabbath Day. Pastor Grey led us in prayer and gave us a lesson with his sermon, followed by the announcements of village news. Outside under a blue and sunny sky the tableboard was filled with smoked cod, smoked meats, coleslaws, bread and bisquits, and many relishes, quiddonies and butters. Baked goods and pies completed our feast and fellowship gathering. It once again felt so good to be at peace and be relaxed. It felt good to be in the village and around people and not be the subject of gossip and whispers and the object of leering eyes! With that thought I am reminded it is our last day in Scituate and tomorrow we go back to Ashville, and Seth.

Our last night in Scituate is as equally beautiful as our day was. Before retiring I opened the window to the sea air, and there was a full moon hanging in the sky over the sea. The sea smoke was starting to roll towards the shore with a cool breeze but still delightful. I know when I return to Ashville I will wish to be here with my children, and I will so miss and long for Olivia, Garrett and Noah, and Jillie, and the feeling of belonging to a happy family.

Olivia and I embraced not wanting to let each other go as Luke, Lyssa and I prepare to journey back to Ashville. She reminds me I always have a home here and she hopes it is soon! Garrett nods and winks in agreement as he lifts the children into the carriage. Jillie has prepared a basket of fresh biscuits and cheeses with some cool tea for our trip back, along with some sweet treats for Luke and Lyssa. As we go down the hill to the village, and pass by the Dalton Mercantile, the Dalton Shipyard, and Sojourn Inn, I am already becoming unsettled and disheartened with worry about returning to Seth.

Our first day home we are greeted by a pleasant summer day. The house is a mess and there is a lot to do. I'm sure it is punishment for leaving here and not staying where I belong! I shall take advantage of the warm day and summer breeze and do so some washing. I gathered the bedding first and filled the pots outside the kitchen pantry with soap and water and lit the fire beneath it. Nicely scrubbed and clean I hung the bedding to dry. The reward for this labor is the smell and feel of a summer day when first getting into a nice fresh bed of linens and blankets to go to sleep. Next the clothing, which most will be put away to autumn, as we can now wear our lighter clothes for the warm season. I am very low on soap but that will have to wait for another day. Seems like there is never enough hours in the day sometimes! Before going inside to prepare supper I enjoy watching Luke and Lyssa merry and gay playing in the meadow. Seth arrived home for supper and tension fills the air as we await his mood. The fact that the children are now walking on eggshells and careful about their behaviors around Seth, reminds me that a decision must be expedited soon!

I was suddenly awoken by the crashing and booming sound of thunder and two children jumping into bed with me. Luke and Lyssa had both been shaken out of slumber by the rumbling of the early morning storm and were frightened. It was a pitch black morning due to the weather except for the flashing light in the sky. Upon rising we all went to the kitchen and lit some candles so we could see and enjoyed a breakfast of coffee, fresh blueberries and johnnycakes with warm honey. It appeared it was going to be a long dreary day and I suggested to both children they should find something to busy themselves to pass the day inside. Lyssa wanted to practice her stitching and began working on her sampler. Luke was carving some wood that would soon become a work of art. I had some mending to do and this would probably be a good day to get it done. The dandelion greens I picked yesterday will make a good soup later for supper on this chilly summer rainy day.

As I read aloud to the children before tucking them into bed the rain was still coming down. Once again we were startled by the sound of crashing and booming! Only this time, it isn't the summer storm, Seth has arrived home, in his usual drunken stupor, and swaggered and stumbled into bed. It appears we have gone unnoticed and he quickly passes out and goes to sleep. We all sigh a breath of relief and I keep reading aloud to the children and we all pretend nothing happened. I tuck the children in for the night, and again, I also sleep in the loft for the night.

Another day, and lots to be done as usual. However, we incorporate some fun into our chores today. Luke, Lyssa and I walk to the strawberry patch and fill my large basket with fresh picked ripe strawberries. Luke and Lyssa also fill their tummies with fresh picked ripe strawberries! Their little faces and little hands red with juicy delight they eat strawberries and also take time to run through the meadows and roll down the hill and play. As we walk back to the house with my basket overflowing with sweet summer bounty the children decide to wash their face and hands in the stream. I knew what was coming but let children be children and soon both of them were swimming and playing in the water! I slipped off my shoes and enjoyed the cool stream water running over my feet and delighted in watching my happy children. I plan on making a pie or two with the strawberries and perhaps some jam, and the children have also suggested some strawberries with fresh heavy cream might be tasty after supper tonight. Dear me, I would have thought they already had their fill of strawberries but am happy to comply with their wishes.

Sabbath Day, and we all go to town appearing the happy family. Seth carrying Lyssa, and Luke holding my hand, as we enter the meetinghouse for sermon. After service we all join together outside around the tableboard filled with a summer feast as Pastor Johnson offers a blessing:

"O Lord, our heavenly Father, Almighty and ever-lasting God, who hast safely brought us to the beginning of this day; Defend us in the same with thy almighty power; and grant that this day we fall into no sin, neither run into any kind of danger; but that all our doings, being ordered by thy governance, may be righteous in thy spirit; through Jesus Christ our Lord. Amen."

As usual, after the blessing, we spend the afternoon in faith and fellowship with our neighbors. Not quite the same as we did in Scituate, as I always feel the village fool knowing what people are thinking and whispering about Seth and me, in Ashville.

Why must it be so hot and the air already wet and steamy the day I prepare to make soap! So much to do today! Doesn't seem quite fair we spend much of our time during the fair weather months, preparing for the long cold months. I stacked some wood by the kitchen pantry and brought some wood over and placed it under the iron kettle and lit the logs. Next, the small barrel of lye and barrel of fat to be added to the warm water. Now, stir and stir, and stir. I wipe my face with my apron as the heat of the day and the heat of the fire cause me to perspire. I spooned the creamy mixture into soap crocks for keeping and storing. I checked on Luke and Lyssa and they are happy at play in the meadow. As I began gardening, the air turned quickly cooler, and the sky has darkened the day with huge black clouds. A refreshing rain began to fall and I let it shower over me. The children seeing this must have decided it looked like great fun and have come to join me! Puddles and little streams began to form as the rain came pouring down. Luke and Lyssa have a grand time splashing in the puddles and jumping in the ponding water. As the rain shower passed it left the earth cleaned, cool and refreshed. We also felt refreshed and cool, but the children were definitely in need of cleaning! I took my little mud minions to clean up and provide fresh clothes and do the same myself. Now, prepare supper!

Seth arrived home for supper as Luke, Lyssa and I were finishing eating. Quite unlike Seth to be home for supper, and more unusual was his demeanor. I prepared him a plate and he remained very solemn while visiting with the children while he ate. He avoided making eye contact with me which further heightened my senses something was definitely wrong!

As always I read aloud to the children before tucking them in for the night. Seth remained quietly down below, the only sign he was home was the smoke from his pipe drifting up to the loft. As I stepped down from the loft Seth summoned me to sit down. Still not making eye contact with me and speaking in a small voice, Seth begins to tell me of some trouble in Ashville, and he is involved. Not willing to share any further details he just wanted me to know. I have heard Seth has been involved in some shady business and connected to some unethical people but now he has confirmed it! As if the children and myself, have not been through enough with his blatant womanizing and reputation of a carouser, now this scandal! And more distressing, is his assumption, we are just going to stand by faithfully, as usual! I hung my head in shame, again, even though I have done nothing wrong. There was a knock at the door and I got up to answer, finding two Ashville constables, here for Seth.

Seth was arrested, but allowed to return home until his trial, as he is considered a person in good standing in town and family man. However, scandal after scandal, and secret after secret, are being revealed during the trial. Mother must be rolling in her grave! Father, taken up with the town trollop and lost the family farm, and now her daughter and grandchildren the subject of Seth's scandalous affairs, all court record! I kept myself and the children out of the town village as much as possible. We have already had enough of the finger pointing, sneering stares, and whispers and gossip, even before this scandal! As if this was not enough, I received word Olivia is very ill.

Garrett sent for me and the children and we went back to Scituate. He wanted I could be with Olivia, and also, the children and I could get out of Ashville during Seth's scandal and trial. Luke, Lyssa, and Noah, hugged and played, and were thrilled to be together again. It made my heart happy to see the children at ease and joyful. I, however, was heartsick when I saw our pale and frail, Olivia. Garrett was preparing to set sail to Jamaica and I will stay with Olivia until he gets back. And of course, Miss Jillie, will be here to mind the homestead and family also!

Life as a family again! How Luke, Lyssa, and I love being here in Scituate, and having a normal life! While Garrett was away, Olivia grows weaker every day. But, somehow, we all have a grand time as usual, when we are all together. Jillie went down to the village for needed supplies and returned with some worrisome news regarding Garrett. The Dalton Family has received news of a great quake in Jamaica, causing high seas, and reports of some missing ships! We decided we must not tell Olivia, as she is already in such a weakened state, and we fear she will not be with us much longer. Jillie and I, and the Dalton Family, will support each other and pray for Garrett's safe return. As I lay myself down to rest tonight:

"O, Eternal God, who alone spreadest out the heavens, and rulest the raging sea; We commend to thy almighty protection, thy servant,

Captain Garrett Dalton, and crew, for whose preservation on the great deep our prayers are desired. Guard him, we beseech the, from the dangers of the sea, from sickness, from violence of enemies, and from every evil to which he may be exposed. Conduct him in safety to the haven where he would be, with a grateful sense of thy mercies; through Jesus Christ our Lord. Amen."

By and by, our prayers were answered, and there was no greater sight, than to see Garrett's ship sailing into the wharf, and at home!

"O God, whose mercies cannot be numbered; Accept our prayers on behalf of the soul of thy servant departed, Olivia, and grant her an entrance, into the land of light and joy, in the fellowship of thy saints; through Jesus Christ our Lord. Amen."

I believe she waited for her gallant captain to return before she departed. If ever an Angel walked this earth, it was Olivia. I am honored to have called her, friend, and she will remain in my heart forever. In the days that followed it was also time for Luke, Lyssa and me to return to Ashville. Seth's trial is coming to an end and we awaited the outcome. With warm good-bye's and the promise to visit soon, Garrett, the Dalton Family, and Jillie, remind me, I always have a home with them, in Scituate.

As we arrived home I noticed the leaves are already full of color and am reminded how much there is left to do before winter! I entered the door prepared for the punishment of extra work to do because I went away, in addition to, harvesting, storage of food, chopping and stacking wood, and candles to make. Luke, Lyssa and I settled in and prepared supper. Seth arrived home and seemed genuinely happy to have us home. After supper I attended to my wifely duties while Seth spent some time with the children. Perhaps through all this scandal he has changed his ways but I will not put too much stock in that notion as yet.

I awoke to the first light of day to the smell of coffee and Seth and the children talking. I was a bit surprised Seth was home in the morning. As I entered the kitchen the children and Seth had set the table for breakfast and I began to prepare our meal. Seth announced he would be home for a few days to help with all the chores for the pending winter months. We all enjoyed hot coffee, warm bread and butter with some eggs and fried pork, and sliced baked apples with cinnamon. The children spent the rest of the day at play. Seth smoked meats, chopped and stacked wood, and tended to the field harvesting. I gathered the autumn's bounty from my kitchen garden and herb garden, and spent the day churning butter. Luke and Lyssa have added to the pantry storage adding chestnuts and acorns, along with my baskets of beans, squash, parsnips, turnips and pumpkins. I hung some mint, parsley, scallions and thyme to dry. It has been a very productive day indeed.

It has been a fortnight since Seth has been to the Towne Tavern or Shady Creek Farm. I have not yet determined if he has really changed his ways or on good behavior pending the outcome of his trial. Time will tell. However, I have a deep rooted feeling this is temporary. I don't know if it's a blessing or a curse that the women in my family tend to be very clairvoyant, but, I do know I am usually right about my feelings.

The signs of the winter returning are here. The trees are barren, gray days and frosty mornings. The children are up early and having their favorite breakfast of warm cider and griddled bread with maple syrup. Seth is at work at the Blacksmith shop and my chore today is to finish my candles. Once again I am missing my departed best friend Olivia. We made candles together every year in Scituate with bayberries. Bayberries are abundant around the Dalton's home by the sea and add such a lovely fragrance to the candle. My mind drifts back there and I wonder how little Noah is fairing without his mother, and how Captain Dalton is managing? The Dalton's are such a warm loving family and I know they will be alright, however, we all miss Olivia.

I sat frozen emotionally and physically in the courthouse as Seth's fate was being determined. Seth sits looking at the floor aloof, the Selectman and town Treasurer sit with looks of impending doom on their faces as if they are on trial, the owner of the Towne Tavern is also present, and I once again try to figure out the connection? To add insult to injury the Selectman's hired girl who is also Seth's lady friend has the audacity to be present, along with my father and his girlfriend the town trollop! My whole scandalous life on display in the town square! As the Magistrates enter the room I feel like I'm sinking into a dark deep hole. The deafening silence seemed forever and then finally: NOT GUILTY! As we walked out of the courthouse a gentle snow has begun to fall. We stopped by our friend's to retrieve the children and off we go for home. Home! What a joke! I wondered how long Seth's good behavior would last now that he's a free man. And I also wondered if I would ever really know what had happened? I feel like I know less about this whole trial and scandal than anyone!

After a fashion, and just as I had expected, Seth went back to his usual ways! Luke and Lyssa and I finished our supper and as usual Seth wasn't home. He is most likely at the Towne Tavern or working late again horseshoeing some horse at Shady Creek Farm. Amazing how often those horses need tending too! More amazing is Seth insulting my intelligence believing I don't know what's really going on! I read aloud to the children and tucked them into bed as they fell fast asleep. As I came down from the loft I sat in my chair by the fireplace. Tonight is the night! Enough is enough! I am telling Seth I am divorcing him. Finally, in the early hours of the morning, he came stumbling through the door, as usual, reeking of perfume and alcohol. I told him I was divorcing him and he laughed in my face. In his usual cocky style he told me to go ahead and try it because he gets what he wants in this town! I answered I was going to try it, I'm done being afraid of him, and now he knows! As I went to go back up into the loft and sleep with the children he grabbed me by my hair and threw me to the floor. I should have known better to approach Seth when he is drunk and send him into a violent rage! I ran out into the barn to take the fight and the noise away from the children. They have been through enough. Seth followed me to the barn and once again threw me to the ground. There was cow dung where I landed and Seth proceeded to rub my face in it. He stomped out of the barn and locked the barn doors from the outside. I have never been so humiliated and violated in my life. I prayed and prayed through the night that I would survive and not freeze to death.

"Oh God, merciful and compassionate, who art ever ready to hear the prayers of those who put their trust in thee; Graciously hearken to me who calls upon thee, and grant me thy help in this my need; through Jesus Christ our Lord. Amen."

As I drifted in and out of sleep I dreamed about Olivia and at times felt warmth around me. Morning finally came and I awoke to find the barn doors open and my Mother walking away! How could that be? Mother is dead! I ran after her! Outside the barn doors the only footsteps in the snow were my own. I thanked our Lord for my survival through the night and sending me my own special Angels to watch over me.

I went inside the house and first washed the tears and dried cow dung from my face. I packed up Luke and Lyssa's belongings and mine. The children awoke and I fed them a quick breakfast of warm porridge with molasses, some bread with strawberry jam, and coffee. After breakfast I bundled them up and we all got in the wagon and left. As we were traveling to town I thought it strange the children were not even asking why we had all our belongings with us and what was happening? I believe they know. Children know what's going on in their homes even if they don't talk about it. We arrived at Pastor and Mrs. Johnson's home and we went inside. We would stay with them until I divorced Seth. I also sent word to Scituate and Captain Dalton we were now definitely in need of a home if they could help.

Our time spent with Pastor and Mrs. Johnson was like a real home. The children were peaceful and happy and so was I. I feared they would miss their father, but, remembered Seth was never home anyway, so it wasn't much of an adjustment not to have him around. Mrs. Johnson kept the children as Pastor and I went to court for the hearing on my divorce. I am so fearful as women have no rights in divorce cases as they own nothing and the law states the father of the children claims them as his property also. Especially in this town, as Seth stated the night before I left him, he gets what he wants in this town! Before entering the courthouse Pastor Johnson led me in prayer.

"Almighty God, who sittest in the throne judging right; We humbly beseech thee to bless this court of justice and the Magistrates; and give unto them the spirit of wisdom and understanding, that they may discern the truth, and impartially administer the law in the fear of thee alone; through him who shall come to be our Judge, thy Son, our Saviour, our Jesus Christ. Amen."

"Divorce between Rebecca Allen Thomas and Seth Thomas is hereby granted. The court further grants the two children: Luke Mark Thomas and Lyssa Elizabeth Thomas will remain in the full and sole custody of their mother, Rebecca Allen Thomas. It is hereby granted by this court without prejudice and with the full accordance of the law."

As Pastor Johnson and I walked out of the courtroom, there before me was Captain Garrett Dalton.

The children are settled and at peace since we moved to Scituate. We spend much of our time with Garrett and Noah and the Dalton Family. As promised we will always have a home here. Garrett and I agreed it would be more fitting for me and the children to reside at the Dalton family's owned Sojourn Inn, than under one roof at this time.

The winters are damper and a bit colder here by the sea than in the farmlands of Ashville. The wharves and the town are covered with ice and the days are sometimes cold and gray with the sea smoke rolling in and out like the waves of the sea. However, we have never been so warm, both by the light of the fire log and by the Dalton Family. And never have I felt more safe and secure.

Garrett and Noah are coming to visit and for a meal today. The children love being together and Garrett and I have found we have much in common regarding moral values and life in general. We both abhor any kind of family violence, those who stand in judgment of others and prejudice, and dishonest government. We both enjoy reading and the literary arts and making the world a better place. After a lovely meal in the main dining room of roast duck with acorn and chestnuts, turnip, warm bread fresh from the hearth with butter and quiddones, we adjourned to the parlor. The children were happy at play and Garrett and I enjoyed conversation and warm coffee and being together.

Luke and Lyssa were all tucked in and sound asleep as I spent some time in quiet solace and serenity in my own bedroom. My room overlooked the wharves and the Dalton Shipyard and I love looking out at the sea. Tonight is a beautiful winter night, the full moon is drifting in and out of the fast moving clouds, and a few of the Dalton's ships are gently rocking bare poles in winter sleep, and the street is quiet. I am so grateful to be here and feel as I have finally found a real home.

"Almighty God, Whose loving hand hath given us all that we possess; Grant us grace that we may honour thee with our substance, and remembering the account which we must one day give, may be faithful stewards of thy bounty; through Jesus Christ our Lord. Amen."

Another day at Sojourn Inn. Cook has made us a porridge of warm cornmeal with molasses and scalded milk, topped with nutmeg and cinnamon, pie and coffee. She is awake and working before the rooster crows! Not only has she already prepared breakfast, she has dinner and supper already cooking too. Quahogs nestled in wet seaweed from the morning low tide are currently steaming open over the fire. Salt pork, onion and potatoes will be added to a nice broth along with the quahogs for a hearty soup. Cook also adds heavy cream and it is delicious. She has also prepared a baked pumpkin pudding with ginger, cinnamon and sugar, one of my favorites! After breakfast Luke and Lyssa joined some other children that were staying at the inn in the parlor and were happily at play. I stayed in the kitchen and helped Cook with whatever I could. I am not used to being such a lady of leisure and it felt good to be industrious. A far cry from my life in Ashville. Life here is peaceful and serene and literally delicious. Additionally, we are a part of a loving family. As the snow begins to fall outside Cook has another surprise in her apron pocket. Later we will go outside and gather some fresh fallen snow, pack it and mold it bowl size, and serve frozen with warm maple syrup. Luke and Lyssa will love that! I wish Noah was here to have some too. I wish Garrett was here also. I find myself longing for Garrett's company. I believe I have grown quite fond of our gallant Captain Garrett Dalton and wonder if Olivia would approve?

I sat in the parlor and read aloud to Luke and Lyssa as we awaited Garrett and Noah's arrival. They are having a hard time staying still, as they are excited about our visitors anticipated arrival, and spend more time watching out the large front windows, than on the story I am reading. With a squeal and a jump Lyssa leaped out of the chair, with Luke bolting behind her, as our company arrived. To our surprise and joy, Jillie has also come along for a visit. As usual we have a warm and hearty meal together with lots of conversation, love and laughter. And, as usual, we all adjourned to the parlor. Well, almost all of us. Garrett has asked Jillie to put the children to bed, and with a wink of Garrett's eye, and Jillie's nod and knowing smile, this was done. Garrett took a deep breath, rose from his chair, knelt down in front of me and took my hands in his, and asked if I would consider marrying him, and raising our children together? He did not want an answer promptly, he asked me to think about it and would await my decision.

After a lovely wedding at the Sojourn Inn, Luke, Lyssa, and I moved to the Dalton home with Garrett and Noah. In the front room overlooking the sea, Garrett and I enjoyed a glass of peachy fireside, while the three children slept soundly. We discussed what a year we have just endured, what we have learned from it all, and felt blessed for such a happy ending. We talked about my life in Ashville, the passing of our beloved Olivia, and the tragedy of the Salem Village Witch Trials. Twenty four human lives lost due to prejudice and fear! Several hung, some died in prison, and one poor gentleman was pressed to death by stones. All because a body was thought to worship differently or live differently than others in society. In light of my life in Ashville, our children will never witness family violence in the home! We will teach them this is not acceptable in the home and should never be tolerated anywhere. I myself, will never forget the hardships and cruelty I suffered in Ashville, and no matter how high I may rise in this life, I dedicate my life to always saying a prayer and helping those who are desperate or destitute. We also vow to teach our children to always stand up for and uphold justice, and have no tolerance for greed, dishonesty, or misuse of authority. Prejudicial government must never rule! Jillie will remain living with us, as will the precious memories of Olivia. All of us, under one roof, sharing loving hearts and memories, in a very special place, called home.

LIBERAL

~ *Harmony Waddell* ~

I was abruptly awaken by the shaking of my bed and a crashing sound from my kitchen pantry. Following, was a crash of thunder! As I arose from my bed, and looked out my window, it was clearly a bright and sunny spring day in our little river town. The crash from the pantry was some crockery that was shaken from the shelf and hit the floor. Nothing to be frightened of, quite normal here, and happens from time to time. There are a few legends regarding our crashes and shakes. One is, the Great Spirit "Hobomoko." The native people of these river banks respect and honor Hobomoko, the Thundering God, and call our area, "the land of little noises." Another legend is of some "witches" on both sides of the river. The witches on this side of the river, would cast spells on the witches across the river, causing a great disturbance in the land.

Whatever the rhyme, the reason, or the cause, we are quite accustomed to our "little noises."

It's just past dawn but I can feel it's going to be warm for a spring day. I can see the village of town from my front windows and observe others are also awake and busy. The shipyard is alive with activity, and a few folks are already walking about the Meeting House, The Chandlery, The Mercantile, The Sail Loft, The Sawmill, and Cooperage. The sun has now made a full appearance over the river, and the Riverside Inn and the Legends Landing Tavern, are mirrored in the water as if reflected in a looking glass. Meanwhile, here at my home, the dandelions in my meadow and on my hillside, remind me I need to get busy too. Springtime is when I make my dandelion wine. It's a favorite at Legends Landing Tavern, and with some folks in town.

Two large baskets of dandelions decorate my pantry floor, as I pull out one of my larger pottery crocks. Time to begin! After placing the petals from the dandelions in the crock, and covering with approximately three to four gallons of boiling water, time to seal with a wooden top. It will need to sit for seven days, although will need stirring once a day. On the seventh day, I will need to sieve the liquid into another clean crock, and add sugar that has been boiled down and cooled, lemon juice and the grind from the lemon peels, and add some yeast, and seal for another seven days. Next, siphon to a clean crock, leaving the sediment behind, and add more sugar, and seal for an additional seven days. Then…Dandelion Wine! Siphon into individual pottery bottles. This batch will be ready for the Shad Social. The Shad Social is a springtime event in this little river town. Every year at this time our mighty river is abundant with shad. The fishermen and other folks bring them out of the water filling fishing nets. Outside, by Legends Landing Tavern, the menfolk will prepare the shad on wooden planks, and cook them over an open fire pit. The womenfolk will complete the feast with: baked beans, coleslaw, relishes, and baked breads, and an assortment of pies. As always, at every social gathering, there will plenty of cider, grog, ale, and dandelion wine.

My friend, Laurel, owner of Legends Landing Tavern, has invited me, and other friends to a tea at the tavern, in the parlor, at four o'clock. Laurel is small in stature and large of heart with smiling eyes. The tavern has a reputation for being a bit bawdy, by the well-to-doers of town. It does serve as home and hearth to many a fishermen and shipyard worker, indeed sometimes a rough and rowdy lot, however, Laurel is a lady! Never will a body know hunger or lack shelter as long as Laurel owns this tavern. It puzzle's me why the well-to-doers think they are better than us, when I hear tell, some of the well-to-do women are quite well known by some of our fishermen, and some of our presumed well-to-do gentlemen have been seen sneaking out in the night from the tavern! I arrive promptly at four, and find friends, Heather, Gay, and Carrie have already arrived. Heather is tall and striking and very educated. A women ahead of her time! She is a political writer and has been published in newspapers in Boston, Providence, Philadelphia, and Hartford. She has spent a great deal of time with another political writer, who is well known, her name is Mercy Otis Warren, wife of James Warren, and together they have attended many political meetings and hosted many politicians. Abigail Smith Adams, another dear friend, married to John Adams, who is now our Vice-President, is another lady who speaks on our behalf, reminding Mr. Adams, when writing the Declaration of Independence, to not forget the rights of women! Gay is slight in build and every inch the farm girl. Since her father passed away and her brother died in the war, Gay has been managing the family farm. It is uncommon for womenfolk to be property owners or manage menfolk, but, she has commanded much respect doing so. Carrie is spunky in nature and a bit of a tomboy, but can also appear the proper lady. She is the midwife in our town and has helped bring many of the babies into this world, and has cared for the sick and injured also. All five of us are fiercely independent women, a bit ahead of our time, but not without our beau's. Heather's beau is Samuel, a Harvard man of letters and brilliant, as she. Gay's beau is Issac, and Issac also owns a very large farm in town. Carrie's beau is Benjamin, and who owns the village cooperage. Lance is Laurel's beau who owns the shipyard, where my beau Alonzo works as the carpenter who does all the fine finishing in the Captain's and Officer's quarters of the ships. I am known for my waist long silver hair, my wines and pantry apothecary, and I believe, my eccentricity. As usual, we ladies talked and enjoyed the afternoon away! Dusk has turned to dark and I am glad I remembered to bring a lantern along for my walk home. As I was walking along the laneway by the riverside, something up the river caught my eye. It's quite foggy, but I think I am seeing a ship. The fog is making the ship come and go, or, are my eyes playing tricks on me? I sat down on a large rock on the bank determined to solve this mystery. I put my lantern behind the rock and turned it down low so I could better see. After some time the ship appeared out the fog again, and is closer. It appears ghost like in the fog, but, it's definitely a ship! A sloop, a sloop with a crossbones flag! A chill ran through my body and I wanted to run but curiosity kept me seated. I have heard of this legend, but, thought it was just another yarn of the old salts at Laurel's tavern. The legend is, the ghost ship of Captain William Kidd travels this river. Kidd hid some treasure under a ledge up river at the neck and somewhere right around here, and returns from time to time, in search of his booty. The sloop is now before me, and I can see it is at full sail, and although it remains ghost like in the fog, so noted: San Antonio! I remained frozen to the rock where I sat until I could not see the ship anymore, and then continued on home. As I lay in bed I thought of all the legends of pirates that have sailed our river and eastern coast: John Rockham, known as "Calico Jack," and his lover Anny Bonny, Mary Read who disguised herself as a man, Edward Teach, known as "Blackbeard," ... and Captain Kidd! I will never speak of this except with Alonzo, and my best friends, Heather, Gay, Carrie, and Laurel.

Summer has arrived and I don't believe it can get any hotter than it is today! I chose a fine day to make strawberry wine. The heat from the boiling water in the pots add to the heat of the summer day. I should have known this morning when the sun came up over the river like a fireball setting the river ablaze in reflection that it was going to be a hot day! Strawberry wine is made much the same as the dandelion wine. The strawberries need to be mashed by hand, and then the rest of the recipe is the basic sugar, lemons and yeast. The house started to cool down as I cleaned up and put the pots away. I poured myself some cool water and went out to sit on my front stoop in my favorite rocking chair. The air is a bit hazy due to the summer's heat but I can see down to the village. The shipyard workers are working very hard finishing a sloop and I looked to see if I could see Alonzo. Lance's shipyard was not as large as others up and down the river, like Clark and Markham, or Gladding and Wooster, but, he turned out some fine ships. I leaned back in my chair and rested my eyes. I must have fallen asleep because the next thing I knew I was awoken by big wet raindrops splashing my face. Black clouds hovered above me and the wind was picking up. Just as I got inside a bolt of lightning lit up the dark sky and the sound of the thunder rolled down the river. It became so dark I had to light a lantern. The wind grew fierce and is slapping the rain against the house. All of a sudden, on my roof top, and against my glass, was a sound of rat-a-tat-tat, ping-pang, bing-bang! It sounded as if someone was throwing tiny stones at the house. I looked outside and small balls of ice were bouncing off the ground and hitting the river so hard it looked like a boiling pot! The storm passed quickly leaving cool fresh air, the smell of clean earth, and a horseshoe of pastels in the sky over the river. The birds started chirping away as if telling all in the woodland and riverbank it was safe to come out. I am tired as it has been a long and industrious day and I think I shall have some tea and a biscuit and retire early.

Gay, Carrie, and I were enjoying an afternoon tea at Heather's house. Laurel was unable to make it today as the tavern often keeps her very busy. Heather's house, like Heather, is always warm and inviting and welcoming. After tea, we adjourn to the library filled with books and a harpsacord in the corner. We ask Heather to play for us, and she chose to play some music from two of her favorite composers, Johann Sabastian Bach and Wolfgang Amaddeus Mozart. Then, interesting conversation regarding the current events and the state of affairs of our country was always a favorite topic to be enjoyed, especially with Heather. The four of us have a lovely afternoon, as usual.

The sloop at Lance's shipyard has long last been completed and Lance is hosting a party at his home tonight. Tomorrow will be the blessing of the ship which all the townfolk usually turn out to celebrate. Alonzo and I arrive at the party and find everyone merry and gay. Present are Heather and Samuel, Gay and Issac, Carrie and Benjamin and many others. Laurel has left the tavern in the hands of her tavern girls, Maggie, Irene, and Annie, and is busy hosting the party with Lance. A grand time was had by all at Lance's beautiful home that overlooks the river and the shipyard, with the newly finished ship in view.

I awoke at first light, tired from the party, but, excited about the blessing of the Judith Lee, the newest ship on the river! The sun was burning the fog off the river and clearing the village for a festive day. A good sign! There are a lot of superstitions surrounding shipbuilders, captains, sailors and crew, and fishermen. To share a few:

GOOD LUCK: Always have the ground blessed where the ship is going to be built. Build north to south in direction, if possible. Start building on a fair day, good tide, and westerly wind. Place a gold coin or silver coin in the keel. Moon waxing (new beginnings) or full. Wednesday is a good day to begin. Woden, the God of the forest, would be in favor of this day. Always name and bless the ship before sailing. Step on board right foot first. And the best day to set sail is Sunday.

BAD LUCK: Never use black walnut wood, it attracts lightning. Never start building on the 13th of the month. Never start building or launch on a Thursday, Thor's day, God of storms. Never start building or sail on an east wind or heavy surf. Never begin a voyage on a Friday. Never change the name of a ship, and never step on board left foot first.

Pastor Brown arrived and joined us all in blessing the Judith Lee. The blessing, some prayers, and cheering and we all went to Legends Landing for a celebration! Our mighty river and river towns are well known for our shipbuilding, sea captains and merchants. There is a lot of trade up and down the river, and along our eastern coastline, and across the waters to the West Indies. Not far from here is the mouth of the river where the river flows to the sea.

The darkness of the morning and the rain gently tapping my window pane made me want to sleep just a bit longer. However, the anticipated excitement of the 4th of July day celebrations was enough to make me rise and shine. Independence Day is a huge celebration and social gathering in our patriotic river town. I dressed quickly, had a small breakfast, collected my blueberry pie for the social, and made my way down the laneway to the village. The rain has stopped as if by request and the sun is shining brightly as I join Alonzo and the others at the Meeting House. Pastor Brown led us in prayer, followed by a hymn, and the ringing of the meeting house bells! Ringing out freedom just as the liberty bell in Philadelphia. As we proceed outside the Fife and Drum Corps were ready to lead the way to the meadow by the riverside, for the social. We all enjoyed the music, especially the children, who march along to the beat of the drums and sound of the fifes. Before engaging in food and fellowship the flag is raised. Pastor Brown shared the meaning of our flag in full detail: The stripes are red and white, and the thirteen white stars on the blue background represent our united thirteen colonies, in a circle to show our equality. The red is for valor and hardiness. The white is for innocence and purity. The blue, for vigilance, perseverance, and justice. Next, the thirteen gun salute. One shot fired for each united colony. Now, food and fellowship! The tableboard was filled with a delicious summer bounty of creamed salmon, summer harvested fruit and vegetables, baked goods and blueberry pies. A full day of celebration followed with a riverside bonfire. Alonzo walked me home and I bid him goodnight at my stoop. Before going inside I took one more look down at the village, and noted, the red embers from the bonfire swirled upwards toward the dark blue sky filled with shining white stars! Red, white and blue! Lest we never forget how fortunate we are to live in this land of the free!

As I enjoy some time of relaxation at my favorite spot on my stoop overlooking the village and the river, I relish the last of the summer days. The days are growing shorter and the air is cooler in the evening, hinting autumn is not far behind. The scampering about of a few chipmunks and squirrels gathering acorns remind me there is much to do to prepare for the long cold months ahead. I need to spend some time out in the woods and riverbank myself and collect some roots, tree barks and plants for my wines and pantry apothecary. The hillsides are beginning to show colors of yellow, and shades of orange and red, and add to the color of the approaching evening sunset in amber glow over the river. The katydids are singing an autumn song and the gentle breeze rattles the drying leaves of the trees…sounds of the season. Tomorrow I am going to Gay's and help with the harvesting at the farm so I best be getting in to my bed and get some rest. Before retiring I gave one more glance to the river and village and spy one of the fisherman sneaking into the back door of one of the well-to-doers! One of the well-to-doers whose well-to-do sea captain husband is out at sea presently! The same well-to-doer who also has me discretely deliver wine to the same back door!

It is a brisk day but the sun warms my face as I walk to Gay's farm. I make my way passed the pond where I share the laneway with a gaggle of geese also making their way. A few ducks are gliding across the water as if greeting me, and just by chance, a fish also makes itself known by jumping out of the water and back in with a splash. As I get closer to the farmyard I can hear the mooing of the cattle and the cluck cluck clucking of the hens. The horses are prancing and dancing in the lower meadow and the farm hands are busy bringing in hay and corn from the fields. Gay is waving in the front door of the farmhouse as I arrive. I juggle my many baskets as I enter her kitchen and hand her a few bottles of wine. She usually sends me home with baskets of farm fresh foods and harvest goods every year and I bring her wine in fair trade exchange and friendship. Farming is a lot of work and it takes many hands to get the work done. Gay has been doing an excellent job managing operations of the farm. As much as our river town prospers with our shipbuilding, merchants and artisans, farming is also our stock and trade. We all must eat! Gay and I share a laugh as we talk about how the well-to-doers think they are better than us in social standing, viewing us as commoners, we who work with our hands. Do they not realize that they may not be well-to do if not for those of us who work with our hands? We share an added laugh as we suppose if Issac ever musters the courage to propose marriage to Gay, together they will own almost half the town in land.

After a very busy day in Gay's kitchen I have baskets full of jellies and quiddones, preserved vegetables and fruits, some smoked meats, and a loaf of fresh home hearth bread. Additionally, because of my bountiful baskets and day has turned to dusk, Gay has had one of the farmhands bring a horse and wagon to the door to escort me home. He is a very nice young gentleman by the name of Zachary. Zachary and I spoke of farm life, the weather, and the coming winter as we made our way to my house by the river. Almost to my door he shared a very interesting story that happened at the farm just a few nights back. He heard the haunting howls of coyotes running the ridge behind the farm, probably hunting down a deer for their evening meal, and decided to check on the farm animals before retiring to his bunk in the bunkhouse. As he stepped outside he was met with a pair of glowing eyes looking at him from the dark. Startled and ready to run back inside thinking it was a coyote who wandered from the pack, he realized it was a small black fox. He tried waving at it and shouting at it but it didn't move. Unsuccessful at chasing him away Zachary picked up a small rock and threw it at the fox. Without a flinch or even a blink of the eye, the fox sat there eyes glowing in the dark, as the small rock appeared to pass right through him! Zachary decided something was very strange about this black fox and went back into the bunkhouse to get the advisement of another farmhand. Back inside the bunkhouse he learned the legend of the black fox. As the legend goes the black fox has been around for many moons. The natives of the land report arrows shot from their bows would pass right through the animal. The natives honored the black fox and came to regard him a kindred spirit. As years went by and us new people came to the land across the waters, hunters and farmers alike balked at the native's belief of the black fox. However, a few hunters did report taking a shot at a black fox, with the same result. So, anyway, so lives the legend of the black fox. By the end of the telling of the black fox legend Zachary had me safely home and at my door. After thanking Zachary and sending him on his way I had some coffee and a piece of farm fresh bread and warm soup, then went to bed.

Life on the river has much to behold all the seasons of the year, but autumn is definitely the most colorful! The leaves are now bright orange and bright red, and shades of yellows and browns. They fall like raindrops, and swirl and dance, before resting gently on the floor of the woods. As I gather roots, barks, and plants for my pantry apothecary I am surprised by a passing snake! I stop for a moment as he goes peacefully on his way, and I go the other way. I took inventory of what I had gathered so far: elm bark, dogwood, white oak, black birch, ash and beech. A bounty of hemp which is the cure all of most illnesses. As I make my way back through the meadow I gather a few more medicinal plants. Once upon the riverbank, and almost to the laneway, I spot a batch of fairywand and add that to my collection also. As I arrive home I placed my baskets on the stoop and took my place in my favorite spot overlooking the river and the village. As I rested in happy solitude I watched the colors of the season fall to the water and float downriver like a little autumn fleet of ships. I am once again reminded how much I love living here.

Tonight is the annual Harvest Dance at Legends Landing. Alonzo will be by soon to escort me, so I should get ready! As Alonzo and I walk towards the village, we are guided by lantern light and starlight. As we walked to the swooshing sound of the autumn leaves at our feet, we stopped for a moment to behold a large bright orange ball lifting out of the hillside over the river! A full harvest moon! The party had already started as we arrived and we joined the usual cast of characters. Laurel and Lance were both very busy hosting and serving up the cider, wine, rum and ale. Four of the fishermen we know, Sid, Cyrus, Zeb, and Quinten, were well into their grog. Sid was playing the wind whistle as the other fishermen and old salts joined in with their favorite chanties. Nathan, Gabe and Tyler were also present and we greeted them as we passed by. They work with Alonzo at the shipyard, but, right now were more interested in being in the company of the tavern girls, Maggie, Irene, and Annie. Alonzo and I finally find a seat at a table with Heather and Samuel, Gay and Issac, and Carrie and Benjamin. A very festive night at Legends Landing. We were enjoying being together and the excitement of the throng when Issac stood up and asked for a moment of silence. Mind you, it takes more than a moment to quiet this crowd down! Once Issac finally had everyone's attention and our curiosity, Gay also arose from her chair and stood proudly next to Issac. The announcement we all had awaited was received with cheers, whistles and applause! Issac and Gay will be wed this coming summer! Heather has obliged to play a waltz to honor the newly betrothed couple and we moved into the parlor as Issac and Gay danced in celebration. I wonder what the well-to-doers will have to say about this? How will they look down their noses at the couple that owns half the town? Once again, it makes me wonder, why are there people, who really believe they are better than other people? As Gay and Issac finish their waltz we resume to the party back in the tavern.

I put another log on the fire and sat down in my chair by the front window. While I was enjoying my coffee and the first snow of winter, I observed a horse and wagon approaching. As it got closer I could see it was Carrie, and as I opened my front door, she rushed in quite frantically! Carrie asked that I come with her quickly, she needed assistance with a pending new arrival to the village. I ran to my pantry and thought what would be helpful? Fairywand, Elm Oil, Dried Hemp Leaves…let's go! Carrie and I arrived at the home of the soon-to-be parents and I was quickly introduced to the couple: Jo and Steven. Carrie gave Steven a bit of rum to calm his nerves and I got busy brewing some fairywand tea for Jo. Carrie encouraged Jo to sip the tea as it is useful in easing the pain of childbirth. Carrie looked below the belly of the young mommy to check on the progress of the baby's arrival. Carrie then moistened the area with the elm oil ointment to ease the arrival of the baby. Afternoon turned into night, and the night turned into day again. Steven was wearing out the rug with his pacing the floor, and Jo was growing tired and weak from the discomfort of the baby who was taking it's time to join us! I lit some of the crushed hemp leaves and placed them in a small pottery vessel and encouraged Jo to inhale the smoke. It eased the pain and also helped as a sedative. Alas! The baby was ready to make its arrival. A pretty little baby girl! Wait! What? Another baby? Yes, another baby! Arriving also was a handsome baby boy! Twins! Our little river town has been blessed with two new children with the help of Carrie. I so admired Carrie and how kind and compassionate and skillful she was caring for the sick and those in need of medical care. After we got the new family settled, Carrie and I set out to return to our own homes.

Winter was making itself known today with a very heavy and steady snow. The wind is roaring outside and down my chimney. At times the snow became so heavy and the wind blew so hard I couldn't see the river or the village. The storm sent some snowflakes down my chimney into the fire with a spit and a spat on my burning logs. I think I shall not be going anywhere today, nor, do I suspect I will have any callers. A good day to take stock of my inventory.

*ASH/roots- bark: Brew as tea. Good for colic or tummy ache.

*BEECH/bark-leaves: Brew bark in hot water, cool, clean wounds or sores. Brew leaves as a tea, cool/warm, gargle for sore throat. Good as antiseptic.

*BLACK BIRCH/twigs-bark: Brew as tea for relief of rheumatism. Brew, skim oil, apply to aches and pains, soak woolen cloth with brew and wrap on limbs. Good as pain reliever.

*DANDELION/dried leaves: Brew as tea. Good for laxative.

*Dogwood/bark: Brew as tea. Good as fever reliever.

*ELM/bark: Boil in water, skim off oil, cool. Apply to burns or use ointment to aid in childbirth. Use as ointment.

*FAIRYWAND/root: Brew as tea. Good for pain relief in childbirth.

*HEMP/dried leaves: Brew as tea. Inhale smoke of burning leaves. Good for pain relief or sedative.

*LADY'S SLIPPER/root: Brew as tea. Good for sleep aid or sedative.

*WILD CHERRY/bark: Brew as tea. Good for relief of cough.

*WHITE OAK/bark: Brew as tea. Good for relief of diarrhea.

*WITCH HAZEL/bark-twigs: Boil in hot water, cool to warm. Soak cloth in liquid and wrap on aches, pains or itch. Soak cloth in cool water for relief of fever or headache. Good as pain reliever or relieve itch.

*Dandelion Wine. 3 bottles Spirits or Drink

*Elderberry Wine 5 bottles Spirits or Drink

*Strawberry Wine 11 bottles Spirits or Drink

Alonzo has arrived at my door by way of horse and sleigh. It is a beautiful evening and warmer than the usual bitter cold of the season. As if right on cue there is a full moon lighting the way for a romantic sleigh ride. The new fallen snow is a prism of lavender, blue, and pink, and twinkles in the moonlight. As we travel down the laneway almost to the village, the whole world has become a tapestry in pastel. Over the river, up in the sky, along with the full moon, the sky is a hue of green, yellow, red, purple and gold! It is absolutely breath taking! Alonzo said the colors in the sky are called the Northern Lights. We sat in awe of the beauty of it all! After a fashion, we made our way to Legends Landing to warm up for a spell. The snow squeaked underfoot as we walked to the door. All the usual cast of characters, and Laurel and Lance were present. The tavern girls were busy also, or at least Maggie and Irene were, I haven't seen Annie as of yet. Alonzo got us both a mug of mulled cider and we took a seat by the fireside. Lance and Laurel made their way over to visit for a bit. I inquired about Annie's whereabouts as I have only seen Maggie and Irene? Laurel filled me in on the latest news of the town. It appears Annie has taken up with one of the well-to-doers in the village. One of the well-to doers who has left his well-to do wife for Annie! Quite the scandal! One of the old salts chimed in about Connie!

I asked him who Connie was as I haven't met a Connie in town. He said she comes by from time to time. He saw her the other day down by the Seven Sisters Ledge. As the legend goes, Connie, is the local river serpent! She appears long and snake-like with a very long neck. She swims just below the surface of the water and will raise her long neck and head up and look around as she goes, and then will submerge again. And with that, I believe we were caught up on all the local news! Alonzo and I finished our cider and visits about and made our way outside back to the sleigh. Alonzo and I talked all the way back to my house about how lucky we felt to live in this little river town.

The ladies are coming to my house for tea today so I best rise up and get going. I tidied up about and got dressed and set the table. Heather, Gay, Carrie and Laurel arrived all minutes of each other and we had our tea and assorted baked goods. As always serious conversations about life and matters, along with lots of laughter, filled the room. We all have our beau's, but, there is nothing like our time spent together, woman to woman. As we have grown older we have all become quite happy with our lives and really don't care about gossip and the righteous ways of self-important people. We all love living here in the town of "little noises" with its many legends, on the banks of the mighty river that leads to the sea. Common folks like us and the well-to-doers. What we've come to learn the most is it really doesn't matter if you're working class/common folk or a well-to-doer…who you really are, is who you are behind closed doors, not in the town village.

HUMANITARIAN

~ *Lizzie Appleby* ~

Nothing in the air today except an abundance of sunshine and the sound of little girl's laughter. The children are collecting the bright colors of autumn from different trees, and placing them into a pile and jumping into them. It has been over a year now since I came to assist Miss Emily with Harbor House. Before coming here I was traveling the country with other women in the National Woman Suffrage Association, supporting the radical notion and ideology that women should have the right to vote, and the equal rights of men. Miss Emily attended a speech I had delivered on gender equality and women's rights in nearby Boston. She invited me to come visit Harbor House and meet the young ladies who reside here. Harbor House is a lovely estate surrounded with a very large lawn and flower gardens. Also, quite the literary neighborhood, with Ralph Waldo Emmerson, Henry David Thoreau, and Louisa May

Alcott, who have all walked these very same streets. While visiting, Miss Emily shared her thoughts with me, also a supporter of gender equality and women's rights, and her hopes for the young ladies here at Harbor House. Miss Emily started Harbor House after the war. The war and some serious illnesses and epidemics left several children in the area needing homes. She noted boys found home quite readily, especially on farms and with likewise industrious folks. It is assumed boys are worth the investment of education also, worthy then to becoming advantageous respectable citizens, however, girls are still groomed to be, ladies, good wives and mothers, and homemakers! This prompted Miss Emily to start Harbor House for girls. Harbor House encourages education, self-reliance and independence, along with becoming a proper lady! After our visit I corresponded with Miss Emily, regularly, she keeping me up to date with Harbor House and the young ladies, and I keeping her informed of news regarding the women's suffrage movement. It was during this correspondence time that I received word from Miss Emily that she was in need of a new assistant at Harbor House. Her present assistant was marrying and relocating, and she inquired if I would consider the position? After a great deal of thought and consideration, I accepted the position, and found it a wonderful opportunity to engage in promoting women's rights and still remain somewhat active in the suffrage movement through correspondence, speeches and writing. And now, as I sit here watching our young ladies leaping and jumping and merry and gay, I am reminded, I made the right decision.

At this time, there are nine of us living here at Harbor House: Miss Emily, our cook Miss Corinne, Rachel, Nancy, Meg, Prudence, and twins Holly and Molly, and myself Miss Lizzie. Rachel, Nancy and Meg are approximately close in age and becoming quite the young ladies. Our little girls, are Prudence, and Holly and Molly. Regardless of any of our ages we are all excited with anticipation of an upcoming costume party!

It is a perfect autumn evening, not too warm not too cold, as we walk to the home where the costume party is underway. It is a grand home with an enormous parlor, all decorated in autumn fare. Cornstalks, and pumpkins and gourds, and two large buckets of water with bobbing apples, and a lovely table filled with cider, doughnuts, and candied treats for the festive occasion. All the girls joined in playing games, dancing and singing. The party ended with a costume parade and all the guest introduced themselves as the character they portrayed. Miss Emily and I stood proudly, as our girls had decided to portray women they would like to emulate:

Rachel: "I am Susan B. Anthony. I am an American Social Reformer. I have dedicated myself to the equal rights of women and would someday like the right to vote in our country."

Nancy: "I am Sybil Ludington. Everyone has heard of Paul Revere, but, I too, rode my horse through my area towns and warned of the British invasion during the Revolutionary War."

Meg: "I am Sacagawea. I am a native in this land and am skilled in the knowledge of the land and survival. I guided two people on a long journey."

Prudence: "I am Sojourner Truth. I was born into slavery and became free. I dedicate my life to God and being a humanitarian, and helping the disadvantaged."

Molly: "I am Harriet Tubman. Some folks call me Moses. I helped to lead my people to freedom by something called the Underground Railroad."

Holly: "I am Dorothea Dix. I was a nurse during the Civil War and now I am working for the proper treatment for the insane and mentally sick. I believe everyone who is ill should have humane and caring treatment."

Miss Emily and I were moved to tears! Our hearts filled with pride and joy for our remarkable young ladies! We are starting to make a difference with our teachings! Our hope is, that someday all children in this country, female or male, grow up in the land of the free, where there is liberty, and justice for all!

The colors of autumn have now passed and the limbs of the trees are bear. The nights are longer and the days shorter, and the coolness of the air reminds me winter is near. Miss Emily and Miss Corinne are taking charge of our ladies for a fashion, as I have been called upon, at a lyceum, in Connecticut, to deliver my speech on women's rights, to an organized forum. I awaited my turn to take the platform and note the large number of men and women in the crowd. I am hopeful this is a sign of positive change regarding the discussion of striving for women's rights in this country. I took a deep breath as I took my place on the platform:

"Good evening. My name is Lizzie Appleby. I stand before you in support of gender equality and for the rights of women in this country. A country that proclaims: "unalienable Rights, that amoung these are Life, Liberty and the pursuit of happiness…" A country that proclaims: "We the People of the United States…" WE! WE the people of the United States. At this time, WE the women, who make up half the people of the United States, are now requesting our "unalienable rights!" Unalienable meaning, what cannot be taken away nor denied! At this time, half of the people of this country, are denied advancement in education, are denied fair earnings, and fair treatment in commerce.

WE, the women, half the people in the United States! Furthermore, at this time, women are bound in a legal system where they have no voice in the laws of this country. At this time we are not allowed to vote! WE, the women, half of the people of the United States! "Life, Liberty and the pursuit of happiness…half of the people of the United States, upon entering marriage, become essentially by law, owned! WE, the women, upon entering this union, become the property of our husbands. Any personal property or monies in our possession become the property of our husbands. Any children we shall bear, become the property of our husbands. In this said union, we promise to obey our property owner! All our rights, become the property of the property owner! If you should choose to free yourself from your property owner, you will face chastisement by your property owner, which is legal, at this time, by the laws of this country. The word tyranny comes to mind! Tyranny… meaning unreasonable, or arbitrary use of power and control! Tyranny… which is proclaimed in this country, intolerable. Half of the people of this country are forced to tolerate tyranny, in a legal system where they have no voice. WE, the women, half of the people of the United States. Additionally, if a woman should choose to remain independent, and own property, and have her own earnings, she will still be obligated to pay taxes, and support the country that she has no voice in. A country where she is denied liberty! A country where she is not allowed to vote! I stand before you this evening, asking you, to proclaim, the misogyny and gender inequality in this country, the United States of America…will no longer be tolerated! To proclaim, that ALL the people of this country, regardless of gender, have the "unalienable Rights", that amoung these are…"Life, Liberty and the pursuit of happiness…" to proclaim, that WE, "We the People of the United States", regardless of gender, are entitled to liberty, and justice for ALL! I stand before you, in representation of half the people of the United States. WE…the women…half of the people of the United States! I stand before you, obliged. Thank you."

20 November 1887
Dearest Miss Anthony:

I hope this correspondence finds you well in health and happiness. I have recently returned from the state of Connecticut where I once again delivered my speech on gender inequality and women's rights. I feel it was well received and was encouraged by the number of people who were in attendance. The lyceum was quite full of both men and women. I am in hopeful anticipation our efforts are making a notable difference for change based on the growing number in support of our endeavors. I remain obliged to you and Mrs. Stanton for your tireless leadership and remain dedicated in support of our cause, the equal rights for women in our country!

Most respectfully,
Lizzie Appleby

I awoke to the sound of gay merry making and the smell of nutmeg, cinnamon, and ginger, and other delicious aromas. I could hear the voice of Miss Corinne and identified the cheerful glee of each of our young ladies. They have been in eager anticipation of our harvest meal and our Thanksgiving Day celebration, and quite obviously have started early in the day to begin preparations!

We all took our seats at a lovely decorated table with a bountiful feast before us. The girls have made corn dollies for each place setting. The tradition of the corn dollies is as follows: it is believed a spirit lives in the last sheaf of wheat to be harvested. The blades of wheat from this harvest are woven into a corn dolly and is to be kept until it is time to plant seeds again. In the spring the dolly will be planted into the ground of the spring harvest as a blessing for a bountiful crop. At this time, we are ready to bow our heads and give thanksgiving to our bountiful autumn harvest. The turkey, dressing, cranberries, vegetables, warm bread, and gravy filled our body, and love filled our hearts and spirits. Before we have our pies and sweets the girls have a presentation prepared as to what they are thankful and grateful for. This year they have prepared quotes from our literary neighbors that speaks to them personally.

Rachel: "The creation of a thousand forest, is in one acorn." -Ralph Waldo Emerson

Nancy: "I have nothing to give but my heart so full and these empty hands." -Louisa May Alcott

Meg: "Rather than love, than money, than fame, give me truth." -Henry David Thoreau

Prudence, Holly and Molly: "Hurrah for the fun! Is the pudding done? Hurrah for the pumpkin pie." -Lydia Maria Child

Applause, love and laughter filled the room and then we all enjoyed our pudding and pumpkin pie.

10 December 1887
Dearest Miss Anthony:

As always, I am hopeful this correspondence finds you in good health and happiness. I have most humbly enclosed a newspaper clipping of my speech, as it appeared in the Boston Globe. With the winter months upon us I fear I will not be getting about as much or doing much traveling, however, I promise to utilize my time and dedication to the cause through correspondence and publication. Please give my best regards to Mrs. Stanton and her family, and I wish them a merry holiday season. Merry Christmas to you, Miss Anthony, and best wishes for a happy new year.

Most respectfully,
Lizzie Appleby

Miss Emma and the children were gathered in the parlor as I arrived home. They were all attentive and in deep thought with their studies and barely noticed I had come through the door. I continued on to the kitchen where Miss Corinne was busy with luncheon preparations. I noted the horses and sleigh were ready to travel outside, but, before I could inquire, the kitchen was filled with the shrill and joyful glee of excited young ladies! Six young ladies jumping for joy as they searched the pantry for winter wear and their ice skates! Woolen leggings, boots, hats, scarfs, and mittens on, we all climbed into the sleigh. Miss Emma and I brought along some warm blankets and some fire logs, and Miss Corinne made sure we had a basket full of nourishment. Traveling along the snow, the children sang Jingle Bells, and other favorite holiday songs along the way. The pond was full of neighbors enjoying the winter day and we joined in upon arrival. The ladies laced up their skates and were on their way as I added a fire log to the fire, and sat down with Miss Emma and Miss Corinne, and watched the ladies glide across the ice. Rachel, Nancy and Meg enjoy skating arm in arm and holding hands. Prudence, Holly and Molly enjoyed trying to stay upright on their skates and not sliding on their bottoms! By and by the little ones enjoyed being pulled across the ice on a sled courtesy of the older ladies. I hope someday these are the days they will remember and cherish when they remember their days at Harbor House.

The tree was decorated with loving care and a wreath hung on the front door. Evergreen, holly, and red berries decorated tabletops, mantles, and shelves, and green, red and white candles, added to the colors of the holiday season. I do believe Christmas at Harbor House is underway. Tonight is the village green caroling party…and off we go! The girls walked before us singing "Joy to the World" and Miss Emma, Miss Corinne, and myself joined in most harmoniously and lit the way by lantern light. After going door to door singing holiday songs and offering good tidings and cheer to the elderly, invalid, and others, who could not come out to the green, we all gathered at the Grange Hall. Hot chocolate, warm cider, peppermint sticks and baked goods were enjoyed by all and as always our neighborhood fellowship. Upon returning home we all put on our night dresses and turned in for the night. As I lay my head down to rest, low and behold, from the hallway, I believe there are some carolers. As I opened my bedroom door, Miss Corinne, and Miss Emma had opened theirs also, and there in the hallway, Rachel, Nancy, Meg, Prudence, Holly and Molly, stood angelically singing: "Sleep in heavenly peace, Sleep in heavenly peace." For the rest of my days I do not think I will ever hear Silent Night so beautifully performed again! Once again, I lay my head down, and I drifted off to sleep in heavenly peace.

As we enter into the new year of 1888, Miss Emily has granted the children a holiday from their school lessons. They will enjoy their time reading, playing, sewing, in song or dance, or exploring their own creativity. I have been invited for tea with Louisa May Alcott, our neighbor, and my muse. We have discovered we have much in common and I enjoy spending time with her and admire her in many ways, and aspire to be like her. We could spend days talking about our favorite authors and writers such as: Ralph Waldo Emerson, Henry David Thoreau, Robert Frost, Walt Whitman, Charles Dickens, Emily Dickinson, Harriet Beecher Stowe, Margaret Fuller, and the list goes on.

Louisa is also a steadfast supporter of the Suffrage Movement, women's rights, and a true humanitarian. We share our philosophical beliefs and enjoy reading aloud from The Dial as we enjoy our tea and time together. Louisa's father, Bronson Alcott, was very involved with the journal, as were Margaret Fuller, Emerson, and Thoreau. Free thinker's and individuals who believe first and foremost, all people are equal, men and women, and that one should explore life through one's own imagination and intuition, and not depend on pure logic. Explore, be an individual, dare to live in simplicity and self-reliance, and be not afraid to question authority! A philosophy called transcendentalism, a philosophy I have adapted and choose to live by. As the afternoon begins to turn to evening, once again my time with my new dear friend passes too quickly. Before leaving, Louisa asks me if I would consider delivering my speech on women's rights to the people of Concord. Of course I am humbled and honored to be asked by Louisa as I am so inspired by her and so respectful of her as a writer and human being. She said she would make the arrangements and call on me with the date, time, and location. As we end our visit with a friendly embrace I notice Louisa looks so tired. I know she has not been feeling well as of late and like others have become a bit concerned regarding her failing health. She served as a nurse for the Union during the Civil War and has since suffered a chronic illness that appears to wax and wane. However, she remains a remarkable woman and a role model for our time and I predict for some time to come.

25 January 1888
Dearest Miss Anthony:

Tonight I delivered my speech once again to the people of Concord, Massachuetts. The lyceum was filled to capacity with men and women and I feel our number of supporters continues to grow. I was additionally honored to be introduced by Miss Louisa May Alcott who hosted the evening. After my speech Miss Alcott facilitated a group discussion on the topic of the right for women to vote and women's equality which was also well attended. I hope this news is rewarding to you as you and Mrs. Stanton continue to work tirelessly with dedication to the Suffrage Movement. I remain proud to be a small part of this process and look forward to the day we all cast our votes into the ballot boxes across America. Many happy returns of the day to you, Miss Anthony, on your upcoming birthday, February 15th, I hope you take some rest to enjoy the day.

Most Respectfully,
Lizzie Appleby

Alas, February! The long winter months are almost behind us and we will soon be welcoming the return of spring! I look forward to storing away the overcoat, cloaks, and woolens and boots, and spending time out of doors. The young ladies have resumed their school lessons and lessons of the arts, along with the training of etiquette of a proper lady. Be advised, here at Harbor House, the etiquette of a proper lady and lessons of social graces, also includes how to be an assertive independent woman! With Saint Valentine's Day upon us that should serve as a good segue to speak to our older ladies about romantic relationships. It is not all hearts and flowers, it is also about being respected as an equal partner in the relationship. Being a good wife does not require being subservient. Prudence, Holly and Molly will most likely be very busy making our beautiful paper cards and baking up something sweet to eat with Miss Corinne. The Grange will be holding their annual Saint Valentine's Day dance, which Rachel, Nancy and Meg will busy themselves preparing dresses and bows in celebration.

Saint Valentine's Day! Harbor House is always filled with love, however, it is well documented today! Beautifully decorated paper valentines and paper flowers grace the walls of our dining room. Miss Emily, Miss Corinne and myself, have also contributed to the day with chocolate fudge and a valentine for each of our young ladies. They are growing up in an ever changing world, hopefully changes for the human good. If we can teach them and show them understanding, kindness and love, I believe they have the core capacity of a human being to be a positive productive citizen. While it is wonderful for them to believe in love and romance and affairs of the heart, I believe teaching them love in the ways of human kindness and understanding will serve them well in trying to maintain and/or achieve a peaceful society.

March can be a gloomy month with gray skies trying to shed winter and grow spring. But today, the darkness hanging over Harbor House, Concord, and afar, is the news of the loss of our dear departed Louisa May Alcott. I will so miss her, and our times together, sharing our love of transcendentalism philosophy, literature and writing, and views of life and the world. She taught me so much! I wept with uncontrollable grief and a broken heart. I spent the day in my room wanting to be alone and to grieve. Miss Corinne brought a tray of hot tea and biscuits but I had no appetite. Miss Emily stopped by my room before retiring for the day. Day has turned to night and I suppose I should try to get some sleep. As I began to fall into slumber I remembered something Louisa had once wrote and said: "I want to do something splendid…something heroic or wonderful that won't be forgotten after I'm dead…I think I shall write books…" Well, I believe, Miss Louisa May Alcott will not be forgotten. I do indeed believe people will long know her name for generations to come. I promise, I will never forget you!

> It was a mild day for March and I was hopeful spring was arriving early this year. The rain is pounding down, making huge puddles that overflowed into little rivers across the lawn and down the laneway. The children

were a bit restless due to being held up in the house due to the weather, however, Miss Emily was providing grand entertainment in the parlor. Miss Emily played the piano while the ladies enjoyed games of singing and dancing. I entered the room just in time for a rousing chorus of," B-I-N-G-O, B-I-N-G-O," a fun little jingle about a dog named Bingo! The song is sung approximately five rounds, each time dropping a letter to the name, and clapping in the letters place, ending with clapping of the hands five times in rhythm and beat to B-I-N-G-O! A song and dance the ladies find quite entertaining! Next, The Farmer In The Dell! A circle dance and song game, where the farmer starts out in the middle of the circle, and as everyone dances around the farmer chooses a wife to join in the center of the circle. This continues on as the wife chooses a child, who chooses a nurse, who chooses a dog, who chooses a cat, who chooses a mouse, who chooses some cheese, and then the cheese stands alone! It was at this time I went to the kitchen to retrieve Miss Corinne, as she and I were needed to play the game, as the ladies were short two people. Miss Emily cued us with the keys of the piano and a farmer in the middle, and then we danced and sang as we awaited to become the wife, the child, the nurse, the dog, the cat, the mouse, or the cheese!

I awoke in the early hours of the morning to the sound of sleet and ice tapping my window pane. I got out of bed and added a log to the fire and got an extra blanket as it had grown damp and chilly. I thought it rather strange weather as it had been such a mild day yesterday. By first light the temperature appeared to have dropped again as it was now snowing heavily accompanied by a strong and forceful wind! So much for my early spring prediction! We all met down in the kitchen wanting something warm to eat and drink. The whole house had cooled quite a bit during the night due to the howling cold wind. As the children warmed themselves in the kitchen, Miss Emily and I added fire logs to all the fireplaces. The snow continued to fall all day without stopping and was now piled up to the windows. Miss Corinne tried to go out to the wood shed for more fire logs but the kitchen pantry door was forced shut with a snow drift. The wind was blowing so hard at times all we saw outside was a sheet of white! We will have to make do with the wood pile in the outer pantry. As we retired the snow and wind remained relentless. Morning brought more of the same, more snow, and gale force winds! We could not see out of the north side windows of the house as they were covered with snow. Out of the other windows we noted branches, twigs, and pieces of the roof, scattered across the property. Miss Emily, Miss Corinne, and myself, tried to not make a fuss about the storm as we sensed Prudence, Holly and Molly are a bit frightened. Rachel, Nancy, and Meg followed suit and were very helpful distracting the little ones with fun and games. Miss Emily, Miss Corinne, nor I, had ever seen such a snow storm in our lifetime! The snow lightened up by afternoon and the wind had died down to a dull roar. We had decided we would all bring our bedding downstairs to the parlor for tonight, and sleep together in one room to conserve fire logs, using one fireplace for warmth. With what appeared to be twenty foot snowdrifts outside it may be a spell before we get outside for more fire logs.

Days did go by, and though the snow and wind finally stopped, we saw no one anywhere up or down the street. Everyone was snowed in! By and by, we recovered from the snow storm, and it was the talk of the town, and the whole east coast! It had even made the front pages of the newspapers! No one alive had ever seen a winter storm like that!

7 April 1888
Dearest Miss Anthony:

I hope this correspondence finds you well and enjoying the freshness and warmth of spring. I fear I have been slacking in working on our cause since Miss Louisa's passing, and recovering from such a long dreary winter. I seem to be down in the doldrums and lacking motivation. My writing on the cause and correspondence seems to have lost its rhetoric, and I have lost my boldness of delivering my speech. Please, not to worry, I am still faithfully dedicated to working towards the vote for women and making our equal rights known! I am hopeful the warmth of the sun and all that is renewed in spring will help to renew my spirit. My best regards to you and Mrs. Stanton, and all the women of the National Woman Suffrage Association.

Most Respectfully,
Lizzie Appleby

Our young ladies were as gay as the springtime and it is always good to see them happy! As part of the rite of passage of spring, our ladies are painting and decorated cooked eggs with Miss Corinne. Miss Emily and I joined the gathering and helped to decorate our beautiful springtime baubles. The symbolism of the egg, as we have been taught, represents fertility and rebirth. Painting and decorating them represents celebration. Spring is the time of new beginnings and rebirth.

Although many of us who strive and work for the suffrage of women and women rights, correspond with Miss Anthony and Mrs. Stanton, they seldom have time to respond, as they are tasked with the many duties of the forefront. So it was to my surprise I received a correspondence from Miss Anthony:

Dear Miss Appleby:

I hope this correspondence finds you well and feeling better since your last letter. I am fully confident that you will regain your stamina. Please know Mrs. Stanton and I appreciate all you and the others do for the cause. Be well, and I leave you with this thought: "Let my name stand amoung those who are willing to bear ridicule and reproach for the truth's sake, and so earn some right to rejoice when the victory is won." ~Louisa May Alcott

Fondly,
Miss Susan B. Anthony

As I folded the letter and placed it back into its envelope for a forever keepsake, I am once again, impressed and inspired by the intellect and insight of these astounding women! Time to pull myself together and forge ahead as the women I admire do!

Preparations for the May Day Festival have Harbor House in busy and happy excitement. May Day baskets to be made, the young ladies dresses to be finished, and a cake to be made as our contribution to the festivities. This year is very special for us as our own Miss Nancy has been chosen May Day Queen. She will lead the parade to the Maypole, deliver an opening ceremony speech, and then lead the ladies of town in a Maypole Dance. Rachel, Nancy, Meg, and myself, are on assignment gathering wildflowers for the May Day baskets. The little girls, Prudence, Holly and Molly are making candies for the baskets with Miss Emily, and Miss Corinne is in charge of the cake. As we arrive back to Harbor House with our arms full of flowers, the smell of a freshly baked cake fills the air, and baskets with candies are awaiting the flowers on tabletop. We complete the baskets with gay colored ribbons and then helped the young ladies with their dresses and hair.

We arrived at the Concord Tavern where the crowning of the May Day Queen will begin the festivities. All the young ladies of town look so beautiful and ladylike in their white dresses and chatting and giggling fills the air. Nancy was called to the stage and crowned with a wreath of flowers and ordained the May Day Queen of

1888. She couldn't have looked more beautiful! Just over five feet tall, with her doe like big brown eyes, and long dark hair, she appeared a porcelain doll! She delivered her speech with the grace and elegance of a true proper lady and then led us all to the Maypole. We all joined in singing as the ladies held the ribbons and danced around the Maypole, left and right, in and out, with great care and celebration. We ended the festival back at the tavern enjoying punch and cakes and visiting.

Spring was turning to summer and I was called upon once again, to deliver my speech, this time in the state of Rhode Island. I bid all a fond farewell with the promise to return as soon as possible. I was hoping I may also be able to visit the seashore while I was in Rhode Island and surprise everyone with gifts from the sea upon my return.

6 June 1888
Dearest Miss Anthony:

I am happy to report to you that I am well and back to diligently working on our cause. I have just returned from the state of Rhode Island, where I spoke before a multitude of supporters. After speaking, I was invited to tea by a writer from the Providence Daily Journal, who is now in possession of a copy of my speech, and pledges to publish it. I will forward you a clipping promptly upon my receipt. Additionally, upon learning of our young ladies here at Harbor House, this journalist and gracious gentleman, has offered us the use of his summer home in Watch Hill. We are presently very excited with anxious anticipation of our holiday at the seashore! My best regards to you and Mrs. Stanton.

Most Respectfully,
Lizzie Appleby

It is a picturesque summer day on the seashore, as we arrive in Watch Hill, Rhode Island. The summer home of our generous new friend is a lovely and grand Victorian with scalloped trim and seaside piazza! Prudence, Holly and Molly, can barely contain their excitement and long to put their feet in the sea. Rachel, Nancy, and Meg, promise to watch over the little ones, while Miss Emily, Miss Corinne, and I unpack, and off they go running bare feet to the sea! Unpacked and dinner prepared, the children return to the house with all the news of the seashore! Miss Emily, Miss Corinne, and myself, could not get a word in edgewise, while we heard news of a lighthouse, a carousel with flying horses, a big yellow house that's a hotel and sells ice cream, waves, seashells, starfish, and boats, and more! It had been a long day of traveling and excitement and the girls went to bed early. Miss Emily and Miss Corinne chose to spend some quiet time in their bedrooms, but, I heard the sea calling! I walked bare feet to the water's edge and walked along the sea and the foam. I found some large rocks and sat awhile. The whole area felt strangely familiar, however, I know I have never been here before. It was an odd feeling, but not in a frightful way, it was actually a very welcoming and peaceful feeling. I feel very much at home here!

Everyone was awake and up at dawn and ready to enjoy another day at the seashore! Today, by unanimous vote, our first stop is the lighthouse. As we arrived on the grounds of the light, we were met by a nice woman, by the name of Sally. Miss Sally showed us all around the light and told us all about the assiduous and unflagging duties of a lighthouse keeper. Prudence then inquired where the man was who worked the lighthouse? Sally informed Prudence and all of us, Captain Jared Starr Crandall, who was her husband, and has passed away, kept the light for many years, but now she keeps the light. The young ladies were in awe and inspired that a lady can run and operate a lighthouse! As a matter of fact, Miss Sally, is the first lady to run the Watch Hill Lighthouse. Miss Sally further informed them, ladies can do whatever they want, and should try. I personally adored Miss Sally's answer! Miss Sally further shared there is another lady lighthouse keeper nearby, and her name is, Ida, Ida Lewis. I am sure they will change their minds several times over the years, but, at this time, we have three future lighthouse keepers: Prudence, Holly and Molly! We thanked Miss Sally for sharing her time and lighthouse with us and moved on to the flying horse's carousel. It is indeed a quaint and beautiful carousel. The horses are hung from the top of the carousel, and as it goes around, the horses swing outward appearing to fly. In the corner is a ring dispenser and as you go by you grab a ring in hopes of getting the brass one, which entitles you to a free ride! Music played by a hand- cranked organ completes the enjoyment of this magical and wonderful carousel. After a ride, and Miss Corinne's, brass ring free ride, we placed our hats on our heads and put on our white gloves and went to the Ocean House Hotel for a treat.

Our last night at the seashore! Miss Emily was reading in the parlor, Miss Corinne was enjoying a quiet cup of tea in the kitchen, and the young ladies were sound asleep after another busy day by the sea. It was a gorgeous summer evening complete with a radiant full moon! Once again, the sea was calling, and I again answered the call. I walked bare feet along the sea and foam to the rocks where I sat before. The moon was shining a path of twinkling diamonds from here to eternity and the waves gently washed over the stones and shells in melodious calm. The strange feeling came over me again like a hug from the universe welcoming me home. I sat for a long time taking in the beauty of my surroundings. As I arose to return back, the sea tossed a small stone at my feet. The granite in the stone sparkled in the moonlight and upon closer inspection I found it was shaped like a heart. I thought it a gift from the sea representing love and light, and decided to keep it as a talisman, a remembrance of my love for this place by the sea.

As has been an age old custom, all who live under one roof tend to start the day congregated in the kitchen. Presently, all who live at Harbor House, are honoring that tradition. Miss Emily and Miss Corinne are busy packing picnic baskets with food and drink, complete with red, white and blue linens, for today's July 4th celebration in Concord. The young ladies are merry and gay and ready for a day of food, fun, and fireworks. While everyone will be busy celebrating freedom in throng, I have chosen to spend the day in solitude and relaxation. Funny, how some people regard solitude as being lonely, as I have always found solitude a great freedom! A quiet time to collect my thoughts and contemplate my philosophical wanderlust and serendipity. I have never been one for conformity! As all depart, Miss Emily turns and gives me a knowing look and a wink of her eye. She has the innate ability to read people and I am sensing she is aware of my recent restlessness. My commitment to the suffrage movement, women's rights, and humanity, has been fueled since becoming an avid student of transcendentalism and the philosophy of civil disobedience. I seem to have found my calling...and it is calling!

My farewell party was heartwarming and well attended. I will indeed always carry in my heart and soul, Harbor House, and Miss Emily, Miss Corinne, Rachel, Nancy, Meg, Prudence, and Holly and Molly. Without a doubt, I will visit whenever passing near the area. Additionally, I will take the memories and the life lessons of Louisa May Alcott, and her contemporaries. As I verbally convey these emotions in my farewell speech and expressions of gratitude, I was honored with a resounding response from my guest: "I'll vote for that!"

MERMAID, PILGRIM, LIBERAL, HUMANATARIAN, FREE SPIRIT

~ *Lisa Allen Thompson* ~

MERMAID

Once upon a time I was a mermaid/In the sea way down below/Tales and sea-lore tell about us/But only mermaids really know/ Only mermaids know the real story/Of life way down below the sea/For centuries we've kept our secret/Sisters of the Mermaid Society/ However, yes, we have been seen/By folks in schooners, boats, and ships/And yes for sure my human friends/Indeed, we really do exist/ We've been known to swim ashore/Our favorite time full moons/And together sit upon the rocks/ Melodiously singing mermaid tunes/ Next time you're by the ocean/On some warm summer night/You may hear our sweet songs/Or maybe see us in the moonlight/ Tales and sea-lore tell about us/But only mermaids really know/Once upon a time I was a mermaid/In the sea way down below.

BLUE MOON

It's the mojo bag of nights/The mystical blue moon/If you believe in magick/In the enchantment of full moons/ Cast a spell with harm to none/Use positive energy and white light/Make a wish upon a star/The blue moon is mojo night/ Trusting in the Law of Three/Use practical magick mixed with love/What goes around comes around/The blue moon mojo shines above/ If you believe in magick/In the enchantment of full moons/It's the mojo bag of nights/The mystical blue moon.

REINCARNATION

I practice yoga and reiki healing/And meditation too/I believe in the power of prayer/Crystals, herbs, and organic food/ I live by the Law of Three/A child of the universe I choose/I draw my power from the moon/And the beautiful sea of blue/ Peace, love and white light/Is the magick that I use/And some scriptures from the Good Book/And perhaps a psalm or two/ I live my life on the right hand path/Although I'm sometimes ridiculed/I embrace the vision of my intention/To myself and others I am true/ You know…just a few centuries ago/Me and some others were also ridiculed/At Gallows Hill, in Massachuetts/ In 1692.

FLOWER CHILD

A part of me will always be/A die hard flower child/The times keep right on changing/But they haven't changed my style/ I still believe peace has a chance/And there's a better way than war/If everyone would try together/And care enough…rich and poor/ I still don't care for phonies/

The in crowd or being hip/I don't like being lied to or about/And I don't care for hypocrites/ I still listen to music every day/And I still dig poetry/ Country, Rock, Motown, Folk/It's all solid gold to me/ The times keep right on changing/But they haven't changed my style/A part of me will forever be/A die hard flower child.

DEAR MOM & DAD

As far back as I remember/I was your rebel one/I had a mind of my own/ And my own way to get things done/ And lately I've been thinking/ About the years gone by/The people and the places/And the way I feel inside/ I remember my belief for social justice/And the times I marched for peace/Freedom, love and human rights/And other things that I believe/ Life moves swiftly onward/Things change and things stay the same/Me, I've gone through many changes/But my rebel ways remain/ It seems I've always picked the hard way/In everything I've ever done/ So I guess I'll always and forever/Be your rebel one!

NINE TO FIVE

I'm not cut out for nine to five/Not now and never will be/I'm not putting down the ones who are/I'm just saying it's not me/ I'm just a moving rolling stone/The freelance type I guess/Living the way that I want to/Is what I do the best.

CROOKED TOWN

There was a crooked man/Who walked a crooked mile.../Who had some crooked friends/With the same crooked style/ The crooked men made connections/And together they are bound/And they all work together/In a little crooked town.

HOMELESS AMERICANS

There are Americans in this country/Homeless on the streets/It's an economic problem/And it's gone beyond belief/ The rich get richer and the poor get poorer/It's a growing disease/Now a national epidemic/ Americans in the street/ Janie was a living doll/Her high school junior prom queen/John was the all American boy/Captain of his football team/ They married and had two children/Their American dream was complete/Until hard times hit them unexpectedly/Now their living in the streets/ Dear Mr. Politician/Better take a look around/At this economic problem/Pulling some good folks down/ Bobby went to Paris Island/Back in sixty-six/From there he went to Viet Nam/And did a ten month hitch/He fought for this country/So we could live in peace/Now he's home without a job/Living in the streets/ Dear Mr. Politician/Better take a look around/At this economic problem/Pulling some good folks down/ There are American's in this country…homeless on the streets…

FARM AID

The farmer is in trouble/And we'd better answer the call/Because if the farmer goes down/We're all going to fall/ The backbone of America/Is the working class woman and man/Who take pride in their work/And who love this land/ The crops grown last season/Cost more to grow/ Than the farmer got paid/When the harvest was sold/ When the food prices went up/It was the middle mans gain/But the farmer who grew the food/His income stayed the same/ The farmer needs a fair price/In the market place/The man who now feeds you/Can't survive nowadays/ The farm crisis today/Will be the food crisis tomorrow/When you can't afford to eat/It will be too late for sorrow/ When you can't feed your kids/And you're hungry too/You'll wish you answered the call/That affects me and you…

REBEL CHILD

There's been a lot said lately/About youth today gone wild/Every time you turn around/There's another rebel child/ They're living in the cities/They're living in small towns/They're boys and girls…rich and poor/And they need to be found/ What makes a child a rebel?/What makes them cold and hard?/What makes them do the things they do?/And what makes them the way they are?/Well, have you ever been looked down on?/Have you ever been really scared?/Have you ever watched your dreams die?/And felt like no one cares?/Tommy Johnson was a young boy/When his dad just up and walked away/And now his mom works sixty hours a week/To keep the rent and the bills paid/Tommy grew up fast and tough/Because the reality he found/Is survival is three times harder/On the poorer side of town/Then again, Whitney Tyler was born to wealth/And had all that money can buy/The best clothes, best cars, a silver spoon/But an empty ache inside/ Whitney turned to booze and drugs/And things I will not mention/Giving into lust mistook for love/Because it gave her some attention/What makes a child a rebel?/What makes them cold and hard?/What makes them do the things they do?/And what makes them the way they are?/Well, have you ever been looked down on?/Have you ever been really scared?/Have you ever watched your dreams die?/And felt like no one cares?/The rebel child needs a chance/They need a helping hand/They need somebody to believe in them/They need somebody who will understand/Yeah, there's been a lot said lately about youth today gone wild…

WALKING THE FLOOR

Another night of walking the floor…Shaking, crying, I can't take this much more…Your cruel words never end/Night after night after night/No matter how hard I try/I don't do anything right!/I reach for a hug/You show me your fist/You love me, you hate me/I don't deserve this!/I don't make enough money/I'm not enough fun/No matter how much I do/Nothing is done!/I'm too boring and quiet/I talk way too much/I'm not home where I'm needed/I don't work enough!/I'm way too possessive/I don't care about you/What in the hell/Do you want me to do?/Night after night of walking the floor…Shaking, crying, I can't take this much more…

I'M GLAD I SURVIVED

She was a free spirit/With nothing to hide/The sky was the limit/Each day of her life/Then she was shot down/Deeply wounded inside/Like a broken winged bird/That could no longer fly/The fall seemed unbearable/The pain made her cry/She knew she'd live through it/But she'd much rather die/Each day she was healing/She'd look towards the sky/Could this wounded free spirit/Give life one more try?/She had been shot down/Slowly healing inside/But the broken wing bird/Would once again fly!/The fall seemed unbearable/The pain made her cry/But the sky is the limit…and I'm glad I survived!

I AM AT PEACE & I AM STRONG

Your constant abuse and many lies/Just about did me in/You almost drove me crazy/In the hell that I lived in/But everything is alright now/Now that you are gone/You can't hurt me anymore/I am at peace & I am strong!/No more abuse and no more lies/I walked out of hell today/My life is mine again/I'm going to be okay/Everything is alright now/Now that you are gone/You can't hurt me anymore/I am at peace & I am strong!

I'M NOT HURT ANYMORE

With my pen in my hand/Mighter than your swords/I release the heartache/I'm not hurt anymore/No more broken heart/No more walking the floor/No more sobbing and crying/No more being ignored/No more of your crazy making/No more slamming doors/No more of your head games/No more cut to the core/No more trying to change you/No more me screaming til hoarse/No more of your anger and hatred/No more you anymore!

DREAMS

I was a student of music and poetry/A study of lyrics and song sheets/I spent a fortune on this education/It meant so much to me/Twenty-four hours a day/Music filled that house of mine/And on a piece of notebook paper/I'd try to make my own words rhyme/Adulthood came way too soon/I was thrown in to the main stream/A "real job," a home, a family/Washed away my little girl dreams/Packed away in my closet/Were notebooks of my rhymes/Posters, tapes, and albums/And trivia of all kinds/I'd pretend it didn't matter/Dreams, songs, poetry/But I was drowning in nine to five/And my dreams were dreaming me/So here I am once again/Music fills this house of mine/And on a piece of notebook paper/I make my own words rhyme.

DREAMIN' ON

When I grew up I wanted to be/A writer of some kind/A lyricist, a poet, maybe an author/I like to make words rhyme/Packed away in my closet/Were notebooks of my rhymes/Songbooks, tapes and records/And music trivia of all kinds/It didn't matter anymore/Or so I made it seem/Packed away so carefully/Old memories and faded dreams/Little girl dreams packed away/But my dreams kept dreamin' me/So, I guess it's now or never/If it's ever gonna be...

LIFE IS KINDA FUNNY

Around 1968 or 1969/In the prime of my youth/My parents didn't understand me/They just were not in the "groove"/Barefooted and in faded jeans/With flowers in my hair/They thought I was a "hippie"/I thought that they were "square"/I'd tell them in plain English/Man stop being so uptight/Just hang loose and stay cool/Everything's outta sight/But they didn't understand me/Because as I walked away/I heard my dad say to my mom/"What the hell did she just say?"/ I just really blew their minds/With the things I'd do and say/And I knew someday when I had kids/I would never be that way!/Now here I am in 1992-1993/With a daughter of my own/The parent of a teenager/And it rocks me to the bone/She wears wild colored baggy "jams"/And long t-shirts to her knees/She has these clip things in her hair/And Reeboks on her feet/So I could better understand/Her generation and life style/I asked if we could sit and talk/And so we "rapped" awhile/She said, Mom I'll give it to you straight/I don't know what you worry about/My life is "totally very awesome"/So like really just "chill out"/You know life is kinda funny/Because as she walked away/I laughed out loud as I thought..."What the hell did she just say?"

LIFE IS KINDA...MORE FUN

The year is now 2010. My daughter has a teenage daughter of her own! Her daughter is all excited about a school dance coming up, where all the kids are going to dress up like rock stars from the "olden days." My daughter asked her teenage daughter who she was going to dress up like? My granddaughter answered: "Cyndi Lauper!" Ahhhhh yes! The "olden days of rock n' roll!" Life is kinda more fun....

TECNO-CHALLENGED

So...my teenage granddaughter just received an Ipod for her birthday. She's sitting at the computer "downloading" and "shuffling" and slicin' and dicin', and everything else the technological modern marvel of recording equipment does!

I remember when I was approximately the same age (No! I didn't walk to school in the snow, uphill both ways! That was the generation before me!) I was thrilled to get my Transistor Radio! You could take your music anywhere you wanted to go…almost. You see getting your Transistor Radio to come in was another story! It kinda resembled the modern day dilemma of the first cell phones…"Can you hear me now?" You walked around until you found that unique spot where you actually heard music coming from the radio. You could take it to the beach, the park, camping, your friend's house, oh, just anywhere! You just had to be able to walk, north…south…east…or west…until your Transistor Radio played music. Then, there you stood, sat, or danced in place, listening to your favorite rock n' roll songs! So, this new technological modern marvel of recording equipment the Ipod, is truly amazing to this Grannie, who has become Tecno-Challenged!

Also, I have a three year old grandson. At this point in time his favorite modern marvel of technology is the Satellite TV! One day while my grandson and I were watching the Satellite TV, he asked me to DVR his favorite show. Shouldn't be that hard right? Wrong? You see…Grannie "scrambled" the Satellite TV, and had not a clue, how to "unscramble" the Satellite TV! Now we have no TV! When Grannie was a little girl TV was not complicated. If you wanted to watch something besides what was on the screen, you had options: you could turn the big dial with the numbers right or left, and have your pick of probably eight or ten shows…if you wanted the sound softer or louder, you turned the little dial to the right for louder, and left for softer…if the picture was not clear, that indicated you needed more tin foil on the antenna of the TV. Simple! So this modern marvel of media equipment, the Satellite TV, with DVR, and so on and so on…is truly amazing to this Grannie, who has become Tecno-Challenged!

Grannie is from the wonder years of LP's and 45's, Reel to Reel Recording, 8 Tracks, Black and White TV, and Transistor Radio's! And my RCA Victrola! And…you know what? I really don't mind being Tecno-Challenged, from the wonder years.

But, wait! The grandchildren just got a Wii and Guitar Hero for Christmas! Rock On! "C'mon kids, show Grannie how to rock n' roll in the tecno-age!"

SURVIVAL

I remember walking into the kitchen and telling my Mom I was running away from home. I was running away from home because my Mom and Dad didn't understand me and they wouldn't let me live the way I wanted to! I was approximately eleven or twelve at the time. My Mom packed me a care package of a tuna sandwich, a cookie, and a thermos of Kool-Aid. (In my Monkees lunchbox and thermos!) I went to my bedroom to pack the more important essentials: my RCA Victrola, some 45's and LP's. I additionally packed some pens and paper because I knew this would be an experience I would write about! I said my good-bye's to Mom, my sister who was more intent with TV than me, and Dad was at work, so I'll write him a letter later when I get settled. They have no idea how much they are going to miss me!

So off I went to live my life of freedom and live life my way! I went to one of my favorite spots, across the brook, up the hill, to the big rock. (You could see the house from there!) I encountered my first hardship within minutes. There was no place to plug in my RCA Victrola! I was not prepared for this kind of hardship! A thunderstorm, maybe, or high winds, rain, or wild animals. But, no music? There is no survival without music!

I'll sing! I sang my little heart out for myself and the free world! Because I could! I was free and living life my way! Except…there is no place to plug in my RCA Victrola…

And, by the way, where is the search team? The news crew? Hello? Anybody? I have been gone a long time now! It's getting dark out and cold and damp. The lights just went on in the house, it must be like about seven o'clock now. And…there is no place to plug in my RCA Victrola!

That's what I remember the most about my first taste of freedom and living life my way, there was no place to plug in my RCA Victrola! A mere child, but, I already knew…I needed music to survive.

And so it remains…

ALL I EVER NEEDED TO KNOW I LEARNED FROM MUSIC

MY ALPHABET…

A Animals, Allman Brothers, Aerosmith

B Byrds, Bon Jovi, Bruce Springsteen, Bob Dylan, Bonnie Tyler, Bonnie Raitt, Bob Seger, Bryan Adams

C Creedence Clearwater Revival, Carly Simon, Carole King, Charlie Daniels Band

D Doors, Donavan, Dusty Springfield, Duane Allman

E Eagles

F Fleetwood Mac

G Grass Roots, Gram Parsons, George Thorogood, Guns n' Roses

H Heart

I I LOVE MUSIC!!!

J J Giels Band, Janis Joplin, Joan Jett, John Fogerty, Johnny Rivers, John Cougar Mellencamp, Jeff Healy, John Prine, Jeff Beck, Joe Perry Project

K KISS, Kid Rock

L Lynyrd Skynyrd, Lovin' Spoonful, Leslie Gore

M Monkees, Marshall Tucker Band, Melissa Etheridge, Motley Crue, MOTOWN

N Nancy Sinatra

O Ozzy Osborne

P Paul Revere & The Raiders, Partridge Family, Pat Benetar, Poison

Q Queen

R Rolling Stones, Ricky Nelson

S Steppenwolf, Stevie Ray Vaughan, Stevie Nicks, Sonny & Cher

T Tom Petty & The Heartbreakers, Tina Turner, Tommy James & The Shondells, 38 Special

U U2

V Van Halen, Velvet Revolver

W Woodstock!

X My Generation!

Y Yardbirds, Young Rascals

Z ZZ Top, Zombies, Zakk Wylde

…many, many, more!

MATH…

Love + Music = Life Life - Music= Death

ENGLISH…

The Rolling Stones, The Yardbirds, The Beatles, Hermans Hermits…

SCIENCE…

Inspiration>creativity<dreams>believe, mix with love, and the result will be good music!

HISTORY…

I was born in 1957. (Harley Davidson also unveiled the Sportster!)

My Mom said I was rockin' & rollin' in my playpen to American Bandstand from birth.

The rest is history…

COUNTRY MUSIC

Another Saturday night, out with our local country band, The Buckshots. After the gig, it was off to the favorite breakfast place...my house! A couple dozen eggs, several pounds of bacon, hash browns, and I don't know how many loaves of bread for toast, and a fifty cupper pot of coffee. The guitar player brought his old flat-top in and is picking out some tunes while we eat breakfast and sing along. The sun is coming up now, and the birds are singing, and we decide we should all try and get some sleep. Most "normal people" are just getting up on a Sunday morning, but, musicians and friends, who had a Saturday night gig, are just going to sleep!

Around one or two o'clock Sunday afternoon everyone appears to be coming back to life. Well, almost everyone. I stumble out to the livingroom where all the usual suspects are draped across chairs, the loveseat, the couch, and across the floor. I tripped over somebody wrapped in a blanket on the floor, step in to an ashtray, spill a left over mug of coffee, fall in to the diningroom, and catch myself and remain standing, as if it was carefully choreographed to work out that way! Well, if anyone was still sleeping, we're all awake now! I look out in the driveway, and note, the usual pick-up trucks, muscle cars, and a few Harley's. The usual Sunday morning at my house! At second glance, I note my brother-in-law, asleep in his truck, cowboy boots sticking out of the driver's side window, and cowboy hat hanging off his mirror. We must have run out of room at the inn! My husband and his buddies are filing out to run to the market for picnic stuff, I'm guessing the band is playing on, and we're in need of food and drink for the day. For the hanger-on-er's who wait, I brew up another fifty cupper pot of coffee and break out the Tylenol. Except, for my brother-in-law, who is now in the house with his buddy, home from the Marine Corp, and they pop open a couple of Bud's they found in the fridge, talking about something about "the hair of the dog" and break out in a Merle Haggard song.

A few hours later a picnic and guitar pull and sing along are underway, and life is good here in the country!

EIGHT TRACKS & SIX PACKS

Just got a country oldies CD/And I'm singin' along/My old country top twenty/Are now my good ol' days songs/ We were eight tracks and six packs/And parties 'til dawn/Man, where did it go?/Time sure did move along/ Remember hayfield keggers?/And tailgate parties in trucks?/Sharin' smokes...shots of home brew/And Boones Farm Wine from paper cups?/ Remember bonfires and camping?/And "the rope" at the lake?/The Casino on weekends/And maybe a date./Remember sing-along parties?/Before karoke became the thing/And dancin' to records?/ And the front porch swing?/We were eight tracks and six packs/And parties 'til dawn/Man, where did it go?/Time sure did move along!/My old country top twenty/Are now my good ol' days songs/When we were eight tracks and six packs/And parties 'til dawn/...When we were eight tracks and six packs...

THE HOMETOWN BLUES AGAIN

I wonder what life would be like now/If in my younger days/I had up and left here/Would I be better off today?/ I wonder what would've happened? I wonder what could've been? I wonder if I should've gone? I got the hometown blues, again!/ I don't mean to sound down hearted/'Cause it ain't been all that bad/And when I really take a look around/I'm thankful for what I have/I have a family that I care about/I have the love of many friends/I have a roof above my head/It's just the hometown blues, again/I got the hometown blues, again/The would've, could've, should've's/And the way it might have been…

BRAND NEW SONG

It's so hard to write/A heart that's been wronged/Same old love… same old life/Same old words…same old song/This guitar knows heart trouble/And these heart strings don't lie/It's been played before/Same old song…different night/Hope this bottle of Jack/Holds out 'til tomorrow/ Gonna be a long night/Writin' heartache and sorrow/Pen and paper and sorrow/My love life on rewind/Getting' tired of this tune/Gotta find a new rhyme…/…So damn tired of this tune…time to try a new rhyme/Guitar restrung and fine tuned/Good bye heartache and sorrow/ Pen and paper in hand-Brand new song tomorrow!/No more writing/A heart that's been wronged/I'm singing a new tune/Broken heart now you're gone.

ROCK

It was a bright and beautiful Saturday morning with the exception that I was on my way to work…on a Saturday! However, it is going to be a rock n' roll Saturday night because after work I will be going out to see my favorite Connecticut rock band, DiamondBack! The old nine to five grind is just the reality of life, and rock n' roll dreams die hard… and I'm an old rock n' roller from way back. So, I'm really looking forward to seeing "the boys" and friends tonight. I stopped by the 7-11, got my coffee and a muffin, and hi ho, hi ho, it's off to work I go. As I pulled out of 7-11 my car was leaning on the passenger side and I heard the sound of whomp…whomp…whomp…thud…you know, the flat tire sound! I said: "Oh shoot!" Of course that's not really what I said! Anyway, lucky for me I am only about one hundred feet from home, so,

I wheel the car back in to the driveway. Being the totally independent woman that I am, I have no fear! I will jack this baby up, throw on that stupid doughnut tire, go to a garage and get a new tire put on, and be a little late for work. No problem. Problem! Remember the good old days when a jack was a jack? Not this build-a-jack I have? Yes, with these modern day vehicles, you have to build the jack! Not only is my tire deflated, so is my totally independent woman ego! So great, now I have to call my son-in-law, the mechanic. My son-in-law the mechanic, who just told me a week or so ago, I should get new tires before I get caught somewhere with a flat! So, I call him. He's on his way. I sit down and drink my lukewarm coffee, and what the hell, have a smoke! So, I'm sitting there drinking my lukewarm coffee and smoking and staying true to my save the earth hippie ways I use my now empty coffee cup for an ashtray. You want me to litter? Problem number two…my save the earth hippie ashtray has caught fire! What next? I'll tell you what next! Of course my son-in-law, the mechanic, pulls up just in time, as I am stomping out my save the earth hippie ashtray, by my flat tire car, with the build-a-jack in pieces laying on the ground! And also along to enjoy the show…my daughter and granddaughter have come along for the ride. This day will get better! Just off to a rough start! Besides being an old rock n' roller, totally independent woman, and save the earth hippie…I am also an optimist! My son-in-law, the mechanic, has a real jack, and changes the tire. Problem number three…I need new front brakes! Fine, fine! I will go get new tires and new front brakes! I will just get to work a little bit later, but it's still OK, DiamondBack doesn't hit the stage until 10PM. New tires, new front brakes. My bight and beautiful Saturday morning has now turned into bright and beautiful Saturday afternoon! I get to work and what to my wondering eyes does appear? My boss! In on a Saturday? Problem number four…I promise to come in again tomorrow and make up my time. She strongly suggested I will stay today until the work is done! Bitch! She clearly does not understand rock n' roll! I telephone my friends, leave voicemails for "the boys" in the band, DiamondBack, no rock n' roll Saturday night for me tonight! As I work in to the night, the telephone rang around midnight...DiamondBack! The gig is awesome, they're rockin' the house, and they're sorry I couldn't be there. They, understand rock n' roll! Before, hanging up the phone, it's passed on to a friend, who keeps the line open, and I get to hear two DiamondBack original songs. As I hung up the phone, this old rock n' roller, totally independent woman, save the earth hippie, and optimist, knows, life rocks!

BROKEN

Another night in Hell! Pushing, shoving, slapping and verbal assault was not enough this time...he went for my record collection! At first I thought it was just a threat, just more of the usual mind-fuck! Then, there it was, snap...snap...snap...broken! One of my favorite LP's! A second one...snap...snap...snap...broken! And another! Snap...snap... snap...broken!

I literally drop to my knees...crying...begging...screaming at him to stop! Snap...snap...snap...broken! Another one!

I curl up in a ball on the floor in fetal position...sobbing...begging him to stop. He is happy now! I am broken.

I get up...and run up the stairs to the bedroom and lock the door behind me!

He follows...he stands outside the locked door...yelling..."Why don't ya write a song about that rock star!" "Write one about me, in case you get rich and famous!" He leaves, walking down the stairs in sarcastic laughter!

I yell back at him, trembling, still shaking and crying..."OK, I'll remember!"

He's out of my life now!

I wrote this book with poems, and songs, and short stories, about my love of music and life.

I remembered!

This is a short story called: Broken!

THE CREATIVE BEING

Things you may want to know before entering into a relationship with a musician, an artist, a writer...any creative being. We are usually married to our craft. I am anyway. Let me explain...It's been my experience a creative being is highly emotional and intense, very passionate about what we do, and very often misunderstood. Fair warning: If my nose is in a notebook or on a piece of paper, with a pen burning across the page...don't ask me...do not ask me, what I am doing! Furthermore, no I don't want to watch TV, go out and do something, eat, drink, talk, walk...I am busy! Stay away from me! What part of this doesn't a non-creative being not understand? Hey! I said, highly emotional and intense, passionate about our craft, and often misunderstood! Once interrupted, it usually goes something like this: "I told you to give me my space when I'm writing! I don't want to go anywhere right now, I am not hungry, I am not thirsty...get away from me!" Then back to my pen and paper. "Shit, shit, shit! Now where was I going with this? Damn him!" I have lost my train of thought! Ain't love grand! The notebook gets thrown to the floor, or perhaps across the room, or may take flight into the stratosphere, depending how highly emotionally intense and passionate this artistic breakdown is. Things you may want to know before entering into a relationship with a creative being.

DÉJÀ VU

Out on Music Highway/The rides been long and hard/I know where you've been/And I've been where you are/ I see you searchin' for traces/ Of what's fallen behind/Following destiny stone blinded/The way it is in your mind/And…I guess now you're wondrin', Just how I knew? Well, my song is your song, Been there too…Déjà vu/I know it's lonely out there/When the roads been too long/Searchin' for something/That might already be gone/And when you're feeling lost/On Blue's Avenue/ Keep straight on Dream Street/It's all mapped out for you/And…I guess now you're wondrin', Just how I knew? Well, my song is your song, Been there too, Déjà vu/My song is your song…Take this one with you.

ACCOMPANY ME

If you want to accompany me/You need to know/I'm easy to love/But I'm hard to hold/'Cause I just keep running/Down life's open road/I gave my soul to music/A long time ago/ My song is my laughter, My song is my tears, My song is my strong will, My song is my fears…The love of my life, And it has been for years/If you want to accompany me/ You need to know/I'm easy to love/But I'm hard to hold/The dreamer inside me/Just needs to be free/I ain't getting' no younger/And time is a thief/My song is my laughter, My song is my tears, My song is my strong will, My song is my fears…The love of my life, And it has been for years/I ain't getting' no younger/And time is a thief…Come along, sing my song, Accompany me.

CRY ME A RIVER

It was a rainy and windy night and I was out at a club with friends enjoying one of my favorite local bands. I noticed a special weather bulletin was making its way across the TV screen at the bar. The news was there was a flash flood warning for our area and everyone was instructed to use extra caution while driving along highways and secondary roads. Additionally, there were reports of trees down, wires down, and power outages. I told my friend that was riding with me I think we should head out, it might take us awhile to get home. I dropped my friend at her house and carefully charted my way home. I drove very slowly as I had already encountered fallen tree limbs and downed power lines. I was detoured twice and knew this was going to be a long ride home. As I was approaching the highway I noticed the bridge I had to cross had a lot of gushing water flowing underneath. There was some water across the road, but, I could see the yellow lines and thought it safe to pass. A car went in front of me and got through with no problem, so I also proceeded across the bridge. However, I experienced firsthand what a "flash flood" is! I had just made it to the middle of the bridge, when my car was lifted up by gushing rising water, and I was car surfing! I was washed off the bridge and was now heading downstream! I have no real recollection what was going through my mind on initial shock, but I know my car was filling up with water… fast! I telephoned 911 with my cell phone and help was on the way. I grabbed my CD cases from the passenger side seat and threw them to the back window as now the water was up to my knees and in my lap! Leave it to me to save the music first! I had heard somewhere that the safest thing to do was stay in the vehicle so the rescue crew could find you, and not get out of the vehicle because you could get swept away in the current. But, as the river water was rapidly rising I thought I should have a Plan B! Just as I put Plan B into action and was about to exit my vehicle, going out the driver's side window to get on the roof, the rescue crew was in sight. I'm saved. I don't know what made me look up at my visor, but, there was one of my favorite CD's…Pride & Glory, by Zakk Wylde. I grab the music and my purse as one of the rescue crew starts to help me out of the vehicle. The rescue worker tries to remove the CD from my hand and throw it back into the vehicle. As I grasp it firmly I say: "Hey, this is one of my favorite CD's! Zakk Wylde, Pride & Glory!" The rescue worker responds with: "I don't think Zakk Wylde or his pride and glory gives a shit if you die in this river tonight!" I was thinking, interesting choice of words! I remained CD and purse in hand, knowing the CD was coming with me, or they could pry it from my cold rigormortis hands! So out of the vehicle I go, with my purse, and, my pride and glory! Back at the fire station I am wrapped in warm blankets and drinking hot coffee. The tow truck has been called to fish my boat made by Chevrolet out of the river and my ride home is on the way. It could have been worse! But, once again…music has always been part of my survival!

NO SALE

Well, here I am again, at another Aerosmith concert! We have some young kids in front of us jumping up and down and having a good ol' rock n'roll time, as we are! (we've just been doing it forty years longer!) At about mid concert, one of our young friends makes an observation. He thinks it's very cool that an older lady like me is an Aerosmith fan. I answered: "How the hell old do you think the band is, kid?" Excuse me, sonny, but you happen to be in the company of some of the many "Blue Army." My toys were in the attic before you were born! Now, I'm thinking great…here I am fifty plus years old, I've stopped drinking, stopped smoking dope, and now, older, sober, and straight, I'm going to get in a brawl at a rock concert! Long live rock n' roll! However, we bonded as Aerosmith fans! My new young friend wants to hear concert stories from "back in the day" and so we shared. He was fascinated that I had Aerosmith on vinal…LP's! I was fascinated he knew what an LP or 45 was! He also wants to know how much money I would sell them for. There's no amount of money, kid! NO SALE! After the concert my new young friend and second generation Aerosmith fan is hot on my heels and still bidding for the LP's. He's trying to give me his cell phone number, and email, as the bidding continues and I finally interrupt and respond: "Sure, and I'll throw my first born in there too!" Is he kidding me? Finally, finally, finally…I say to him: "Why don't we rip your heart out of your chest along with your best memories and put a price on that! Dream On!" My new young friend and Aerosmith fan stands there with a blank look on his face and says: "I don't get it?" I responded: "I know…NO SALE!"

BYE, BYE, BYE, BABY, BYE BYE

I'm crusin' on down to the beach…windows open…CD blasting some good ol' Janis Joplin…The Queen Mother of Rock! I'm belting it out and singing along…"bye, bye, bye, baby, bye, bye"…my mind drifts back to the early 70's…

REHEARSAL:

My neighbor's garage has been transformed to a rock arena. I'm on stage shouting to my rock band: "C'mon! Get serious! Our rock show is tonight!" Everyone is getting ready, Debra, Karen, Alison, Catherine, Joanie, and my sister Lori. I had loaded in earlier with my microphone and RCA Victrola. I'm a bit uptight because some of my girls lack the dedication I have for my rock band and rock show! I'm the lead singer, and I am also in charge of sound, lighting, production and management! So anyway, I give a tug at my mini skirt, stomp across the work bench of the garage, I mean stage! "Rehearsal, ladies!" My sister sits ready to drop the needle on the 45 on my RCA Victrola, my girls are in place, and one, two, three, hit it...."You keep saying you got something for me, Something you call love but confess..." In the middle of my song, my sister, is walking out of the arena! "Home for lunch! Are you kidding me?" "When we become world famous, remember, you went home for lunch!" It appears she is a trend setter because now everybody is going home for lunch! "Quitters...You'll never work in this rock show again!"

SOUND CHECK:

Everybody is back from lunch and hopefully ready to get serious about our rock show! My girls are back on stage, and once again my sister drops the next 45, and I grab the mike: "Billy Ray was a preacher's son..."...We rehearse a few songs and I feel we are ready for the show. I send everybody for a break, and I stay and get out the tickets, the posters, and the programs...I'm also in charge of Public Relations!

SHOW TIME:

We get to stay up late tonight because it's not a school night, and I have a rock show! We still have to close before like nine o'clock though...."What a drag, man!" Our Mom's, Grandmother's, Aunt's, Dad's, family and neighbors pack the garage...I mean the house! The arena! Me and the girls take the stage, and my sister introduces us: "Thank you for coming to my sister's dumb rock show! She made us do it!" Giggles from the band and the crowd! It appears not everyone takes the music business as seriously as I do! As I glare at my sister who has the 45 ready and spinning, and turn and give my girls a look that means get serious…one, two, three, hit it: "You don't own me, I'm not just one of your many toys…" We rocked the house! Our rock show was a hit!

AFTER PARTY:

We load out through the side door and have some punch and brownies and thank our fans for coming! We party in to the night, well, at least until bedtime.

I'm crusin' on down to the beach…windows open…CD blasting…some good ol' Janis Joplin…The Queen Mother of Rock! I'm belting it out and singing along…"bye, bye, bye, baby, bye, bye…

Thank You: Lori, Debra, Karen, Alison, Catherine & Joanie

Thank You: Nancy Sinatra for "These Boots Are Made for Walking"… Dusty Springfield: "Son of a Preacher Man"…Leslie Gore: "You Don't Own Me"…Janis Joplin, for everything you ever recorded, did live, and the memories!

RECORDING STUDIO

Most little girls play House, Nurse, Mommy with baby dolls, I played Recording Studio! I would be in my bedroom with my RCA Victrola, my tape recorder, and all the famous rock bands. In my recording studio!

"Come over baby whole lot of shakin' goin' on…"

I would have loved to been in Memphis, Tennessee, at Sun Records in the good ol' days of rock n' roll! Elvis! Jerry Lee Lewis! Johnny Cash! Carl Perkins! Thank God for those cats!

"Just one more mornin'…I had to wake up with the blues…"

Muscle Shoals Sound Studio! I would have given anything to be at Muscle Shoals in the day! Especially back in the day of Duane Allman!

"…wake up momma…turn your lamp down low…"

Can you imagine? Sitting in or jammin' with the likes of: Duane Allman, Lynyrd Skynyrd, Wilson Pickett, Aretha Franklin, Joe Cocker, J.J. Cale, Tony Jo White, Johnny Rivers, Bonnie Bramlett, or Melissa Etheridge? Even the Rolling Stones recorded at Muscle Shoals! If I could have been there…

"wild horses couldn't drag me away…"

If you asked me to name my favorite recording, I could probably narrow it down to fifty or one hundred or so…but, I guess I would have to say, "Honkin' On Bobo" by Aerosmith. American music at its best, by the best American band, at their best! Can you imagine being present at The Boneyard when that was goin' down?

When I was a little girl I played Recording Studio…

TOUR VAN

It was another Saturday in small town USA, and my rock band and I were getting ready for another world tour! Off we'd go…through the pasture… across the bridge over the brook…to the dirt road…and across the cow lot… where our tour van awaited. To most people it was an old rusted out station wagon with wheels sunk down into the earth that time had long forgotten. But to me and my rock band, it was a tour van! We went all around the world in that tour van! The tours waxed and waned depending on who in the neighborhood wanted to be on the tour. Sometimes I was a solo act, sometimes I had an opening act, and sometimes we were a regular rock fest like Woodstock! We played with all the great rock bands of the 60's. Yeah... we drove anywhere we wanted to go in the world! We were young and free and believed in our dreams. In that tour van we could go anywhere, do anything, and be anybody we wanted to be! Sometimes...I wish I could go back...and walk through the pasture...across the bridge over the brook... to the dirt road...and across the cow lot...to my tour van...

WORKING CLASS ADVOCATE

CHILD

"What do you want to be when you grow up?"

"Ummmmm...a writer, write songs, work in a recording studio, be in a band, work at a job that helps people."

TEEN

"Well, have you thought about your future? What do you want to do with your life...how are you going to support yourself?"

"I'm really into social justice, ya know man, tryin' to make the world a better place! I love music and writing and stuff...ya know like Bob Dylan and Melanie. Can ya dig it? Be out there reaching out to people... if I could find a way to use my creativity and support social justice... that would really be cool! Yeah..."

ADULTHOOD

"When are you going to grow-up? What do you mean you like to freelance? You're never going to amount to anything dreaming your life away! Now get a real job!"

"Sigh..."

DREAM ON

"Lisa, Human Services has been the perfect job for you! You've always been so aware of making positive change and helping people! You have really shown dedication to your advocacy in social justice and human services."

"Thank you! However, I think we need a whole lot more people in Human Services that really give a damn about humans! Not just have a real job and make a living! And I'm personally not giving up on being 'creative' about seeing that come true!"

NO SHAME IN MY GAME

I've been writing since I could hold a pen and rhyme, however, my real job is in the human services field. I currently work with victims of family violence/domestic violence. My clients are my reward not my paycheck, and I am honored when I learn I have really helped someone. I feel I get so much more from them than they do from me! I'm a firm believer in being open and honest, much to some of my supervisor's consternation. Although it does require a college education to do this work, I am also a firm believer, to do this work, and do it well, you are not better than anybody else you serve, you are never better than any human being, period! I use creativity a lot, songs, music, poems, art.... because people relate to real feelings! I also am very honest. I've walked the walk, I just don't talk the talk, never judge a book by its cover. Just because the person sitting in front of you wears a suit, don't assume they are happy and prosperous and have never known hard times. And if you're truly going to have a heart and soul in this field, don't assume the person on the other side of the desk is needy, uneducated, cannot sustain oneself and just looking for a handout!

They are some of the most sustainable survivors you are ever going to meet, they just need some help right now…that's our job to help make that happen! Human Services! People go through hard times! It can happen to anybody…it could happen to you! Don't temp fate standing in judgment!

Been there…Done that: Hid my car because I got the friendly certified letter, pay up or we're coming with the tow truck! (it's written in more legal and specific terms but I'm telling it like it is!) I've exited the highway, dodged down the back roads, because a flatbed had been following me too long, and I won't have the payment for another week!

Been there-Done that: My TV just went ssshhhhhhhhhhhhh…and I have no sound or picture! I call one of my friends in the neighborhood and see if it's just me, or hopefully the wind is just blowing too hard or it's a technical difficulty. Because…I thought I had ten more days to catch up on the bill!

Been there-Done that: My telephone hasn't rung all day! I go to check it and I have a dial tone! Good! Hopefully I will have a dial tone until I can pay my bill!

Been there-Done that: I come home and find that my house is creepy silent! I turn on the light switch…and nothing! I call my best friend next door and she reports there was a thunderstorm and the whole town is out of power. Whew! Not the shut off notice this time!

Been there-Done that: It's Wednesday and I have approximately 1/8 of a tank of gas in my car until Friday. I owe the Angels who watch over me big time! It won't be the first time this baby runs on fumes!

Been there! Done that! I sit on this side of the desk, they sit on the other, and the common bond is……we are all human!

I have also facilitated my share of support groups and workshops. But, you see, I'm not the suit and clickity- clack high heel shoes kinda counselor. Once again, I like to keep it real…much to some of my supervisor's consternation, who prefers we look "professional." Look for me in jeans, a t-shirt, and a jacket, and most likely sandals… boots if it's cold. Most times the t-shirt will reflect a positive affirmation or one of my muses such as Stevie Nicks or Aerosmith. I use music and poetry a lot in my work. Because…. people relate to it…. human feelings! Somebody out there knows how you feel, what you're going through, or at least can relate, because…they wrote about it!

No shame in my game! I feel if you're going to work in the human services field, maybe, you should be able to relate to human beings! Not just have a real job….

HUMAN SERVICES

I am not one you would class sophisticated! However…you can dress me up and take me out! I've attended the most elegant cocktail parties and functions, fund raisers, and formal occasions, all in the name of human services. But, I find I am much more relaxed at a bike rally, charity gig, pig roast or pot luck dinner or BBQ, personally, and for my job in human services! When I was a teenager my Mom called me "Jane." Jane was no random choice, you see at the time the well- known Fonda family had an allegedly high spirited daughter. Once in high school, I supported the civil rights movement, the feminist movement, and human rights and social justice movement, and Mom changed my name to "Gloria." I would hope that needs no explanation! So, I guess it's no coincidence I ended working in the human services field. I do manage to bring my freelance and freedom ideals to work with me! And I am proud to say I am damn good at what I do because I love my job! I love putting my ideals to "work" and helping people! However, I did have one supervisor who disagreed and tried to make a "proper" human services worker out of me! I arrived to work at the counseling office in my usual attire: dress jeans, decent t-shirt, suit jacket and boots, finished off with my love of long scarves. Upon entering I am summoned to the office of my politically correct and proper human services supervisor. She starts out telling me what a great job I do for the agency and what an asset I am to the human services field, and my compassion and dedication have been noted. However, she needs to review "dress code" with me! She goes on to tell me she has high respect and regard for me, and out of work, I am free to live as I choose, she passes no judgment, but.... I can't come to work looking like some "biker chick" or "rock star!" I am totally baffled because I'm not sure why her designer dress, high heels, and designer handbag, makes her a more "professional" human services worker than me? If I want to look like I dress out of Stevie Nick's closet or Joe Perry's wardrobe trunk.... WHAT THE HELL IS IT TO HER! My clients are happy and getting the help they need.... I am providing human services! And as, per usual, my mouth and freelance and freedom ideals took over! "They're all kinds of humans in the human services field! Humans who need help regardless of class, tax bracket, race, religion, sexual orientation or personal beliefs! There is also a place for all of us in the human services field who represent them! (I'm on a roll!) I'm glad that you relate to the country club women, suburban housewives, politically correct, and they receive help and relate to you! And you all feel validated! (I took a breath and continued to roll!) Somebody needs to be here for the "pole-dancers," "hookers," "rocker-biker chicks," and "middle class," and they relate to me! They feel validated! I feel validated in my work working with them! I'm too fucking human to do human services? (potty mouth!) Are you kidding me?" My supervisor sits in silence and collects her thoughts. I am sitting in silence thinking I'm probably going to be collecting the things out of my office and this is my last day of work here. She thanks me for my honesty and shares perhaps we should explore how this diversity in counseling is perhaps indeed very beneficial to the program and the people "we" serve. (didn't I just fucking say that?) And off I go, in my "normal" attire and continue to work in human services.

LEGACY OF A FREE SPIRIT

Definitely not one to conform or be restrained by public opinion… that's me! What I've discovered so far in my fifty-seven years in this life is: I'd rather be badass real than real fake! While I have spent most of my life dreaming about being a writer, like most creative dreamers, you have to maintain a "real job" to make a living while you create and dream. I got into human services because I believed I could make a difference in the world. A positive difference. What I found out was a lot of humans in the human services field need to stop looking down their noses at the humans they are supposed to serve! You are of no service to anyone if you think you are better or above anyone else! I believe I learned more about being human from the humans on the other side of my desk than they ever learned from me! Needless to say… regretfully, I burned out…

The real wake up call for me was working as "service staff." Now I am on the other side of the desk! So far what I've discovered in my fifty-seven years in this life is: there are good and bad in every occupation, and people in general! And currently, there is good and bad in health care workers! I like to feel and take pride in thinking I am a good one, however there are some bad ones. I've seen some bad ones along the way, however I have also worked with the best. But contrary to some ignorant public opinion, we are all not lying, stealing, unscrupulous, uneducated cave-dwellers! Some public opinion, not all public opinion! Having someone look down their nose at you is not pleasant! And I maintain, the arrogance and haughty self-importance of some human beings, that truly believe they are better than some other humans, is in itself ...the real ignorance of humankind! I will demonstrate the kind of human being I will strive to emulate if my creative endeavors become lucrative.

CLIENT:

A client of mine had a friend who often visited and referred to us caregivers as: "the girls," "the staff," and my favorite (insert sarcasm) "the help." While we understand we are "girls," (women!) "staff" and here to "help" it is the derogatory manner and tone in her voice which she used to put us "in our place." One day while the visitor was visiting, my client put her visitor...in her place! She said to her visitor: "I will request you address my friends who help me by their first names, please!" Class! Now, that is class! This is someone who I choose to "look up to" and strive to emulate!

CLIENT:

A client of mine had a friend who often visited and referred to us caregivers as: "the girls," "the staff," and my favorite (insert sarcasm) "the help." While we understand we are "the girls," (women!) "staff," and here to "help" it is the derogatory manner and tone in her voice which she used to put us "in our place." One day while the visitor was visiting, my client noticed I took offense to her visitor's derogatory manners. She said to me: "She is a highly revered friend and considered part of our family and you will respect her!" No class! Now, that is no class! This is someone I will choose not to "look up to" and remember NOT to emulate!

Conclusion:

Once again, if perchance, my dreams come true, and if perchance, my writing becomes a lucrative endeavor, I will remember, to remain a person of human services! If I should neglect this promise, somebody please, knock the real fake out of me, because I would rather be remembered as badass real than real fake! Let my free spirit be my legacy. And in conclusion, this is what I've learned so far in my fifty-seven years in this life, and what I strive to be:

"Regardless of affluence or tutelage, a true scholar of humanities, remains a commoner."

-Lisa Allen Thompson

LEGACY

Someday when I leave this world/When to the Summerlands I go/I hereby make this last request/Put me where the river flows/Put me where the river flows/Set my spirit free/And love and light-peace and harmony/Be my legacy/I'm the shooting star and pisces constellation/I'm the sunbeam and the moon glow/I'm the raindrop and the snowflake/I'm the zephyr and the rainbow/I'm the love and light in your heart/I'm the peace and harmony in your soul/Never far away from you/Or where the river flows/Yes! This will be my last request/When to the Summerlands I go/Someday when I leave this world/Put me where the river flows/Put me where the river flows/Set me spirit free/And love and light-peace and harmony/Be my legacy.

FREE SPIRIT

I was born a Mermaid/Feminist of the sea/I believe in love and light/And peace and harmony/I was born a Pilgrim/Came to this land across the ocean/I believe in freedom of worship/Spirituality and one's own devotion/I was born a Liberal/In the land of the free/I believe in justice for all/Pursuit of happiness and liberty/I was born a Humanitarian/In a civil disobedient nation/I believe in peaceful activism/Social justice and preservation/I've been around for many moons/Made many trips around the sun/And I remain a free spirit/On each and every one.

Human Services Close To My Heart:

NATIONAL DOMESTIC VIOLENCE HOTLINE 1-800-799-7233 www.ncadv.org

TEEN DATING VIOLENCE HOTLINE 1-800-799-7233 www.ncadv.org

BACA- BIKERS AGAINST CHILD ABUSE HELPLINE 1-866-712-2873 www.bacaworld.org

NATIONAL RUNAWAY SAFELINE 1-800-786-2929 www.1800runaway.org

NAMI-NATIONAL ALLIANCE ON MENTAL ILLNESS HELPLINE 1-800-950-6264 www.nami.org

-BRIGHT BLESSINGS-

ABOUT THE AUTHOR

Lisa Allen Thompson is a quintessential free spirit, one who is not restrained by convention or restricted by popular opinion. She is abhorrent to labels that define people or their beliefs, her philosophy being everyone's search for truth is self-evident.

Her passions are music and song, many forms of literature and writing, and commitment to being a humanitarian. She believes every living thing is part of the circle of life and that respect of the entity is key to survival.

Lisa lives in Connecticut; however, she feels at home in all of New England. Her creative works have been published in many newspapers and journals, and well received at public appearances.